OZMA OF OZ

A Record of Her Adventures with Dorothy Gale of Kansas,
the Yellow Hen, the Scarecrow, the Tin Woodman,
Tik-Tok, the Cowardly Lion and the Hungry Tiger;
Besides Other Good People too Numerous to
Mention Faithfully Recorded Herein

By

L. FRANK BAUM

AUTHOR OF THE WONDERFUL WIZARD OF OZ,
THE MARVELOUS LAND OF OZ,
DOROTHY AND THE WIZARD IN OZ, ETC.

ILLUSTRATED BY

JOHN R. NEILL

For Your Knowledge

The Publisher wishes to express appreciation for the contributions made by
Mr. Robert A. Baum, great-grandson of L. Frank Baum.

This edition was originally published in 1907 by
The Reilly & Britton Company of Chicago, IL

This facsimile edition is published by For Your Knowledge,
an imprint of Ann Arbor Media Group, LLC
2500 S. State Street, Ann Arbor, MI 48104

Cover redesign by Steven J. Benedict III
Design and Production team: Mae Barnard, Tina Budzinski,
Lori Holland, and Alison Durham

Printed and bound in the United States of America
by Edwards Brothers, Inc.

ISBN 1-58726-035-2

06   05   04   03   10 9 8 7 6 5 4 3 2

Introduction

f a picture is worth a thousand words, then I wonder what kind of picture a book could make, or a set of fourteen? We seldom think of children's books as being revealing of their authors lives and thoughts, but my great grandfather seems to have been an exception. As you read *The Marvelous Land of Oz*, I am sure you noticed all of the puns and the many references to education and money. All of these came from L. Frank's early life experiences and observations. He simply was following the old adage of "write about what you know," even if he was not aware of it at the time.

As we continue to look at the life of my great grandfather and read through the Oz series, I know you will begin to see this simple connection. A connection which L. Frank did not fully see or understand until later in his life. I know that each time I reread an Oz book, it reveals more of my great grandfather's character and personality.

L. Frank was most likely thinking of doing another stage play when he wrote *The Marvelous Land of Oz*. The characters of the Scarecrow and the Tin Woodman are very much like the actions of Fred Stone and David Montgomery, the two actors who played the parts in the 1902 stage play the *The Wizard of Oz*. Again, L. Frank's interest in the stage comes directly from his early days as an actor and playwright.

By the time he was 25, he had studied elocution, been in numerous amateur productions and had even gone to New York to act as a juvenile under the name of George Brooks. His father went so far as to build an Opera House in the oil town of Richburg, New York. It opened on December 29, 1881 and burned to the ground on March 8, 1882!

Having written several plays by this time, L. Frank, along with his uncle John Wesley Baum, aunt Kate and cousin Genevieve Roberts, formed a theater company and opened with his play, *The Maid of Arran* on March 15, 1882, his twenty-sixth birthday. L. Frank's talents included writing the music and lyrics for the play. He played the lead under the stage name of "Louis F. Baum." The play was quite successful and was taken on the road to Kansas, parts of Canada, and on to New York City.

Shortly before the opening of the play, L. Frank's sister, Harriet Neal, introduced him to Maud Gage, a student at Cornell University, who was visiting the Baums in Syracuse, New York. Harriet had prodded L. Frank by saying that she knew he would just love Maude. Upon being introduced, L. Frank, after a moment of staring, took her hand and said "Consider yourself loved, Miss Gage."

In 1989, I had the privilege of working on a movie for television called *Dreamer of Oz*. It was a film on L. Frank Baum and how the book, *The Wonderful Wizard of Oz*, came to be. This very scene was used in the film and I would like to think Maud's actual reply to L. Frank was, indeed, as it was in the movie. She said, "I take that as a promise, Mr. Baum. Please see that you live up to it."

If ever there was a case for love at first sight, this must have been it. L. Frank Baum and Maud Gage were married on November 9, 1882, at the home of Maud's mother, Matilda Joslyn Gage, in Fayetteville, New York.

I mention this because she was against Maud's marriage to L. Frank at first. The reason was that Matilda Joslyn Gage had helped write the "Woman's Bill of Rights" and along with Elizabeth Cady Stanton and Susan B. Anthony, wrote the first three volumes of *The History of Woman Suffrage*. Wishing to have Maud remain a part of the movement and not leave Cornell; she expressed her objections to the marriage. However, Maud's equally strong will and the threat of eloping, finally won her mother's approval.

In fact, L. Frank and Matilda soon came to admire and respect each other. They had many long discussions on the women's suffrage movement and government. In *The Marvelous Land of Oz*, General Jinjur and her Army of Revolt was L. Frank's way of paling good natured fun at the movement and some of its ideas about women.

When Maud became pregnant with Frank, Jr., their first child, L. Frank stopped acting and they settled down in Syracuse, New York. Needing a new job, L. Frank, along with his uncle Adam Clark Baum, started a family oil business called Baum's Castorine Company. They manufactured a number of products, including axle grease. Strangely enough, Baum's Castorine Company is still in business manufacturing customized greases. The company is now located in Rome, New York.

Frank, Jr. was born December 4, 1883 and was followed some three years later by Robert on February 12, 1886. From the beginning, L. Frank was a devoted husband and father. After Robert's birth, Maud had a long and difficult recovery. L. Frank did not hesitate to take time off from work and stay home with her until she recovered.

L. Frank's devotion to Maud was very much like his devotion to his readers as seen in *Ozma of Oz*. As you read the introduction to the book you will note that L. Frank states he would have to write dozens of books to include all the wonderful ideas sent to him by his young readers. He also states "And I wish I could, for I enjoy writing these stories just as much as the children say they enjoy reading them."

By the time he wrote *Ozma of Oz* in 1907, L. Frank was beginning to understand and accept the meaning of his own words. He most likely wrote *Ozma of Oz* with the intent to continue the series, unlike his thoughts on his first two Oz books.

As you read through the story, I hope the new information I have shared with you on his life, makes your journey more interesting. My great grandfather really outdid himself with *Ozma of Oz*. You will meet many new and interesting characters. Many people consider *Ozma of Oz* his best Oz book, but I will let you decide for yourself!

Ozily yours,

Robert A. Baum

To all the boys and girls
who read my stories-
and especially to
the Dorothys-
this book is lovingly
dedicated.

Author's Note

My friends the children are responsible for this new "Oz Book," as they were for the last one, which was called *The Land of Oz*. Their sweet little letters plead to know "more about Dorothy"; and they ask: "What became of the Cowardly Lion?" and "What did Ozma do afterward?"—meaning, of course, after she became the Ruler of Oz. And some of them suggest plots to me, saying: "Please have Dorothy go to the Land of Oz again"; or, "Why don't you make Ozma and Dorothy meet, and have a good time together?" Indeed, could I do all that my little friends ask, I would be obliged to write dozens of books to satisfy their demands. And I wish I could, for I enjoy writing these stories just as much as the children say they enjoy reading them.

Well, here is "more about Dorothy," and about our old friends the Scarecrow and the Tin Woodman, and about the Cowardly Lion, and Ozma, and all the rest of them; and here, likewise, is a good deal about some new folks that are queer and unusual. One little friend, who read this story before it was printed, said to me: "Billina is *real Ozzy*, Mr. Baum, and so are Tiktok and the Hungry Tiger."

If this judgment is unbiased and correct, and the little folks find this new story "real Ozzy," I shall be very glad indeed that I wrote it. But perhaps I shall get some more of those very welcome letters from my readers, telling me just how they like "Ozma of Oz." I hope so, anyway.

L. FRANK BAUM.

MACATAWA, 1907.

Ozma

List

of

Chapters

List

of

Chapters

The Girl in the Chicken Coop

The wind blew hard and joggled the water of the ocean, sending ripples across its surface. Then the wind pushed the edges of the ripples until they became waves, and shoved the waves around until they became billows. The billows rolled dreadfully high: higher even than the tops of houses. Some of them, indeed, rolled as high as the tops of tall trees, and seemed like mountains; and the gulfs between the great billows were like deep valleys.

All this mad dashing and splashing of the waters of the big ocean, which the mischievous wind caused without any good reason whatever, resulted in a terrible storm, and a storm on the ocean is liable to cut many queer pranks and do a lot of damage.

At the time the wind began to blow, a ship was sailing far out upon the waters. When the waves began to tumble and toss and to grow bigger and bigger the ship rolled up and down, and tipped sidewise—first one way and then the other—and was jostled around so roughly that even the sailor-men had to hold fast to the ropes and railings to keep themselves from being swept away by the wind or pitched headlong into the sea.

And the clouds were so thick in the sky that the sunlight couldn't get through them; so that the day grew dark as night, which added to the terrors of the storm.

The Captain of the ship was not afraid, because he had seen storms before, and had sailed his ship through them in safety; but he knew that his passengers would be in danger if they tried to stay on deck, so he put them all into the cabin and told them to stay there until after the storm was over, and to keep brave hearts and not be scared, and all would be well with them.

Now, among these passengers was a little Kansas

The Girl in the Chicken-Coop

girl named Dorothy Gale, who was going with her Uncle Henry to Australia, to visit some relatives they had never before seen. Uncle Henry, you must know, was not very well, because he had been working so hard on his Kansas farm that his health had given way and left him weak and nervous. So he left Aunt Em at home to watch after the hired men and to take care of the farm, while he traveled far away to Australia to visit his cousins and have a good rest.

Dorothy was eager to go with him on this journey, and Uncle Henry thought she would be good company and help cheer him up; so he decided to take her along. The little girl was quite an experienced traveller, for she had once been carried by a cyclone as far away from home as the marvelous Land of Oz, and she had met with a good many adventures in that strange country before she managed to get back to Kansas again. So she wasn't easily frightened, whatever happened, and when the wind began to howl and whistle, and the waves began to tumble and toss, our little girl didn't mind the uproar the least bit.

"Of course we'll have to stay in the cabin," she said to Uncle Henry and the other passengers, "and keep as quiet as possible until the storm is over.

For the Captain says if we go on deck we may be blown overboard."

No one wanted to risk such an accident as that, you may be sure; so all the passengers stayed huddled up in the dark cabin, listening to the shrieking of the storm and the creaking of the masts and rigging and trying to keep from bumping into one another when the ship tipped sidewise.

Dorothy had almost fallen asleep when she was aroused with a start to find that Uncle Henry was missing. She couldn't imagine where he had gone, and as he was not very strong she began to worry about him, and to fear he might have been careless enough to go on deck. In that case he would be in great danger unless he instantly came down again.

The fact was that Uncle Henry had gone to lie down in his little sleeping-berth, but Dorothy did not know that. She only remembered that Aunt Em had cautioned her to take good care of her uncle, so at once she decided to go on deck and find him, in spite of the fact that the tempest was now worse than ever, and the ship was plunging in a really dreadful manner. Indeed, the little girl found it was as much as she could do to mount the stairs to the deck, and as soon as she got there the wind struck her so fiercely that it almost tore away the

"UNCLE HENRY! UNCLE HENRY!" CALLED DOROTHY

skirts of her dress. Yet Dorothy felt a sort of joyous excitement in defying the storm, and while she held fast to the railing she peered around through the gloom and thought she saw the dim form of a man clinging to a mast not far away from her. This might be her uncle, so she called as loudly as she could:

"Uncle Henry! Uncle Henry!"

But the wind screeched and howled so madly that she scarce heard her own voice, and the man certainly failed to hear her, for he did not move.

Dorothy decided she must go to him; so she made a dash forward, during a lull in the storm, to where a big square chicken-coop had been lashed to the deck with ropes. She reached this place in safety, but no sooner had she seized fast hold of the slats of the big box in which the chickens were kept than the wind, as if enraged because the little girl dared to resist its power, suddenly redoubled its fury. With a scream like that of an angry giant it tore away the ropes that held the coop and lifted it high into the air, with Dorothy still clinging to the slats. Around and over it whirled, this way and that, and a few moments later the chicken-coop dropped far away into the sea, where the big waves caught it and slid it up-hill to a foaming crest and then down-

The Girl in the Chicken-Coop

hill into a deep valley, as if it were nothing more than a plaything to keep them amused.

Dorothy had a good ducking, you may be sure, but she didn't loose her presence of mind even for a second. She kept tight hold of the stout slats and as soon as she could get the water out of her eyes she saw that the wind had ripped the cover from the coop, and the poor chickens were fluttering away in every direction, being blown by the wind until they looked like feather dusters without handles. The bottom of the coop was made of thick boards, so Dorothy found she was clinging to a sort of raft, with sides of slats, which readily bore up her weight. After coughing the water out of her throat and getting her breath again, she managed to climb over the slats and stand upon the firm wooden bottom of the coop, which supported her easily enough.

"Why, I've got a ship of my own!" she thought, more amused than frightened at her sudden change of condition; and then, as the coop climbed up to the top of a big wave, she looked eagerly around for the ship from which she had been blown.

It was far, far away, by this time. Perhaps no one on board had yet missed her, or knew of her strange adventure. Down into a valley between the waves the coop swept her, and when she climbed another crest the ship looked like a toy boat, it was such a long way off. Soon it had entirely disappeared in the gloom, and then Dorothy gave a sigh of regret at parting with Uncle Henry and began to wonder what was going to happen to her next.

Just now she was tossing on the bosom of a big ocean, with nothing to keep her afloat but a miserable wooden hen-coop that had a plank bottom and slatted sides, through which the water constantly splashed and wetted her through to the skin! And there was nothing to eat when she became hungry— as she was sure to do before long—and no fresh water to drink and no dry clothes to put on.

"Well, I declare!" she exclaimed, with a laugh. "You're in a pretty fix, Dorothy Gale, I can tell you! and I haven't the least idea how you're going to get out of it!"

As if to add to her troubles the night was now creeping on, and the gray clouds overhead changed to inky blackness. But the wind, as if satisfied at last with its mischievous pranks, stopped blowing this ocean and hurried away to another part of the world to blow something else; so that the waves, not being joggled any more, began to quiet down and behave themselves.

DOROTHY AFLOAT IN THE HEN-COOP

It was lucky for Dorothy, I think, that the storm subsided; otherwise, brave though she was, I fear she might have perished. Many children, in her place, would have wept and given way to despair; but because Dorothy had encountered so many adventures and come safely through them it did not occur to her at this time to be especially afraid. She was wet and uncomfortable, it is true; but, after sighing that one sigh I told you of, she managed to recall some of her customary cheerfulness and decided to patiently await whatever her fate might be.

By and by the black clouds rolled away and showed a blue sky overhead, with a silver moon shining sweetly in the middle of it and little stars winking merrily at Dorothy when she looked their way. The coop did not toss around any more, but rode the waves more gently—almost like a cradle rocking—so that the floor upon which Dorothy stood was no longer swept by water coming through the slats. Seeing this, and being quite exhausted by the excitement of the past few hours, the little girl decided that sleep would be the best thing to restore her strength and the easiest way in which she could pass the time. The floor was damp and she was herself wringing wet, but fortunately this was a warm climate and she did not feel at all cold.

The Girl in the Chicken-Coop

So she sat down in a corner of the coop, leaned her back against the slats, nodded at the friendly stars before she closed her eyes, and was asleep in half a minute.

The Yellow Hen

strange noise awoke
Dorothy, who opened her
eyes to find that day had
dawned and the sun was
shining brightly in a clear sky.
She had been dreaming that she
was back in Kansas aga n, and
playing in the old barn-yard with
the calves and pigs and chickens all
around her; and at first, as she rubbed
the sleep from her eyes, she really imag-
ined she was there.

"Kut-kut-kut, ka-daw-kut! Kut-kut-
kut, ka-daw-kut!"

Ah; here again was the strange noise that had
awakened her. Surely it was a hen cackling!

The Yellow Hen

But her wide-open eyes first saw, through the slats of the coop, the blue waves of the ocean, now calm and placid, and her thoughts flew back to the past night, so full of danger and discomfort. Also she began to remember that she was a waif of the storm, adrift upon a treacherous and unknown sea.

"Kut-kut-kut, ka-daw-w-w—kut!"

"What's that?" cried Dorothy, starting to her feet.

"Why, I've just laid an egg, that's all," replied a small, but sharp and distinct voice, and looking around her the little girl discovered a yellow hen squatting in the opposite corner of the coop.

"Dear me!" she exclaimed, in surprise; "have *you* been here all night, too?"

"Of course," answered the hen, fluttering her wings and yawning. "When the coop blew away from the ship I clung fast to this corner, with claws and beak, for I knew if I fell into the water I'd surely be drowned. Indeed, I nearly drowned, as it was, with all that water washing over me. I never was so wet before in my life!"

"Yes," agreed Dorothy, "it was pretty wet, for a time, I know. But do you feel comfor'ble now?"

"Not very. The sun has helped to dry my feathers, as it has your dress, and I feel better since I laid my morning egg. But what's to become of us, I should like to know, afloat on this big pond?"

"I'd like to know that, too," said Dorothy. "But, tell me; how does it happen that you are able to talk? I thought hens could only cluck and cackle."

"Why, as for that," answered the yellow hen thoughtfully, "I've clucked and cackled all my life, and never spoken a word before this morning, that I can remember. But when you asked a question, a minute ago, it seemed the most natural thing in the world to answer you. So I spoke, and I seem to keep on speaking, just as you and other human beings do. Strange, isn't it?"

"Very," replied Dorothy. "If we were in the Land of Oz, I wouldn't think it so queer, because many of the animals can talk in that fairy country. But out here in the ocean must be a good long way from Oz."

"How is my grammar?" asked the yellow hen, anxiously. "Do I speak quite properly, in your judgment?"

"Yes," said Dorothy, "you do very well, for a beginner."

"I'm glad to know that," continued the yellow hen, in a confidential tone; "because, if one is going to talk, it's best to talk correctly. The red rooster has often said that my cluck and my cackle were quite perfect; and now it's a comfort to know I am talking properly."

"I'm beginning to get hungry," remarked Dorothy. "It's breakfast time; but there's no breakfast."

"You may have my egg," said the yellow hen. "I don't care for it, you know."

"Don't you want to hatch it?" asked the little girl, in surprise.

"No, indeed; I never care to hatch eggs unless I've a nice snug nest, in some quiet place, with a baker's dozen of eggs under me. That's thirteen, you know, and it's a lucky number for hens. So you may as well eat this egg."

"Oh, I couldn't *poss'bly* eat it, unless it was cooked," exclaimed Dorothy. "But I'm much obliged for your kindness, just the same."

"Don't mention it, my dear," answered the hen, calmly, and began pruning her feathers.

For a moment Dorothy stood looking out over the wide sea. She was still thinking of the egg, though; so presently she asked:

"Why do you lay eggs, when you don't expect to hatch them?"

"It's a habit I have," replied the yellow hen. "It has always been my pride to lay a fresh egg every morning, except when I'm moulting. I never feel like having my morning cackle till the egg is properly laid, and without the chance to cackle I would not be happy."

"It's strange," said the girl, reflectively; "But as I'm not a hen I can't be 'spected to understand that."

"Certainly not, my dear."

Then Dorothy fell silent again. The yellow hen was some company, and a bit of comfort, too; but it was dreadfully lonely out on the big ocean, nevertheless.

After a time the hen flew up and perched upon the topmost slat of the coop, which was a little above Dorothy's head when she was sitting upon the bottom, as she had been doing for some moments past.

"Why, we are not far from land!" exclaimed the hen.

"Where? Where is it?" cried Dorothy, jumping up in great excitement.

"Over there a little way," answered the hen, nodding her head in a certain direction. "We seem to to be drifting toward it, so that before noon we ought to find ourselves upon dry land again."

"I shall like that!" said Dorothy, with a little sigh, for her feet and legs were still wetted now and

THE YELLOW HEN

then by the sea-water that came through the open slats.

"So shall I," answered her companion. "There is nothing in the world so miserable as a wet hen."

The land, which they seemed to be rapidly approaching, since it grew more distinct every minute, was quite beautiful as viewed by the little girl in the floating hen-coop. Next to the water was a broad beach of white sand and gravel, and farther back were several rocky hills, while beyond these appeared a strip of green trees that marked the edge of a forest. But there were no houses to be seen, nor any sign of people who might inhabit this unknown land.

"I hope we shall find something to eat," said Dorothy, looking eagerly at the pretty beach toward which they drifted. "It's long past breakfast time, now."

"I'm a trifle hungry, myself," declared the yellow hen.

"Why don't you eat the egg?" asked the child. "You don't need to have your food cooked, as I do."

"Do you take me for a cannibal?" cried the hen, indignantly. "I do not know what I have said or done that leads you to insult me!"

"I beg your pardon, I'm sure Mrs.—Mrs.—by the

way, may I inquire your name, ma'am?" asked the little girl.

"My name is Bill," said the yellow hen, somewhat gruffly.

"Bill! Why, that's a boy's name."

"What difference does that make?"

"You 're a lady hen, are n't you?"

"Of course. But when I was first hatched out no one could tell whether I was going to be a hen or a rooster; so the little boy at the farm where I was born called me Bill, and made a pet of me because I was the only yellow chicken in the whole brood. When I grew up, and he found that I didn't crow and fight, as all the roosters do, he did not think to change my name, and every creature in the barn-yard, as well as the people in the house, knew me as 'Bill.' So Bill I've always been called, and Bill is my name."

"But it's all wrong, you know," declared Dorothy, earnestly; "and, if you don't mind, I shall call you 'Billina.' Putting the 'eena' on the end makes it a girl's name, you see."

"Oh, I don't mind it in the least," returned the yellow hen. "It doesn't matter at all what you call me, so long as I know the name means *me*."

"Very well, Billina. *My* name is Dorothy Gale

—just Dorothy to my friends and Miss Gale to strangers. You may call me Dorothy, if you like. We're getting very near the shore. Do you suppose it is too deep for me to wade the rest of the way?"

"Wait a few minutes longer. The sunshine is warm and pleasant, and we are in no hurry."

"But my feet are all wet and soggy," said the girl. "My dress is dry enough, but I won't feel real comfor'ble till I get my feet dried."

She waited, however, as the hen advised, and before long the big wooden coop grated gently on the sandy beach and the dangerous voyage was over.

It did not take the castaways long to reach the shore, you may be sure. The yellow hen flew to the sands at once, but Dorothy had to climb over the high slats. Still, for a country girl, that was not much of a feat, and as soon as she was safe ashore Dorothy drew off her wet shoes and stockings and spread them upon the sun-warmed beach to dry.

Then she sat down and watched Billina, who was pick-pecking away with her sharp bill in the sand and gravel, which she scratched up and turned over with her strong claws.

"What are you doing?" asked Dorothy.

"Getting my breakfast, of course," murmured the hen, busily pecking away.

"HOW DREADFUL!" EXCLAIMED DOROTHY

"What do you find?" inquired the girl, curiously.

"Oh, some fat red ants, and some sand-bugs, and once in a while a tiny crab. They are very sweet and nice, I assure you."

"How dreadful!" exclaimed Dorothy, in a shocked voice.

"What is dreadful?" asked the hen, lifting her head to gaze with one bright eye at her companion.

"Why, eating live things, and horrid bugs, and crawly ants. You ought to be 'shamed of yourself!"

"Goodness me!" returned the hen, in a puzzled tone; "how queer you are, Dorothy! Live things are much fresher and more wholesome than dead ones, and you humans eat all sorts of dead creatures."

"We don't!" said Dorothy.

"You do, indeed," answered Billina. "You eat lambs and sheep and cows and pigs and even chickens."

"But we cook 'em," said Dorothy, triumphantly.

"What difference does that make?"

"A good deal," said the girl, in a graver tone. "I can't just 'splain the diff'rence, but it's there. And, anyhow, we never eat such dreadful things as *bugs*."

"But you eat the chickens that eat the bugs," retorted the yellow hen, with an odd cackle. "So you are just as bad as we chickens are."

The Yellow Hen

This made Dorothy thoughtful. What Billina said was true enough, and it almost took away her appetite for breakfast. As for the yellow hen, she continued to peck away at the sand busily, and seemed quite contented with her bill-of-fare.

Finally, down near the water's edge, Billina stuck her bill deep into the sand, and then drew back and shivered.

"Ow!" she cried. "I struck metal, that time, and it nearly broke my beak."

"It prob'bly was a rock," said Dorothy, carelessly.

"Nonsense. I know a rock from metal, I guess," said the hen. "There's a different feel to it."

"But there couldn't be any metal on this wild, deserted seashore," persisted the girl. "Where's the place? I'll dig it up, and prove to you I'm right."

Billina showed her the place where she had "stubbed her bill," as she expressed it, and Dorothy dug away the sand until she felt something hard. Then, thrusting in her hand, she pulled the thing out, and discovered it to be a large sized golden key —rather old, but still bright and of perfect shape.

"What did I tell you?" cried the hen, with a cackle of triumph. "Can I tell metal when I bump into it, or is the thing a rock?"

"It's metal, sure enough," answered the child, gaz-

ing thoughtfully at the curious thing she had found.
"I think it is pure gold, and it must have lain hidden
in the sand for a long time. How do you suppose
it came there, Billina? And what do you suppose
this mysterious key unlocks?"

"I can't say," replied the hen. "You ought to
know more about locks and keys than I do."

Dorothy glanced around. There was no sign of
any house in that part of the country, and she
reasoned that every key must fit a lock and every
lock must have a purpose. Perhaps the key had
been lost by somebody who lived far away, but had
wandered on this very shore.

Musing on these things the girl put the key in
the pocket of her dress and then slowly drew on her
shoes and stockings, which the sun had fully dried.

"I b'lieve, Billina," she said, "I'll have a look
'round, and see if I can find some breakfast."

Letters in the Sand

Walking

a little way back from
the water's edge, toward
the grove of trees, Dorothy
came to a flat stretch of white
sand that seemed to have queer
signs marked upon its surface,
just as one would write upon sand
with a stick.

"What does it say?" she asked the
yellow hen, who trotted along beside
her in a rather dignified fashion.

"How should I know?" returned the
hen. "I cannot read."

"Oh! Can't you?"

"Certainly not; I've never been to school,
you know."

"Well, I have," admitted Dorothy; "but the letters are big and far apart, and it's hard to spell out the words."

But she looked at each letter carefully, and finally discovered that these words were written in the sand:

"BEWARE THE WHEELERS!"

"That's rather strange," declared the hen, when Dorothy had read aloud the words. "What do you suppose the Wheelers are?"

"Folks that wheel, I guess. They must have wheelbarrows, or baby-cabs or hand-carts," said Dorothy.

"Perhaps they're automobiles," suggested the yellow hen. "There is no need to beware of baby-cabs and wheelbarrows; but automobiles are dangerous things. Several of my friends have been run over by them."

"It can't be auto'biles," replied the girl, "for this is a new, wild country, without even trolley-cars or tel'phones. The people here havn't been discovered yet, I'm sure; that is, if there *are* any people. So I don't b'lieve there *can* be any auto'biles, Billina."

"Perhaps not," admitted the yellow hen. "Where are you going now?"

The Letters in the Sand

"Over to those trees, to see if I can find some fruit or nuts," answered Dorothy.

She tramped across the sand, skirting the foot of one of the little rocky hills that stood near, and soon reached the edge of the forest.

At first she was greatly disappointed, because the nearer trees were all punita, or cotton-wood or eucalyptus, and bore no fruit or nuts at all. But, bye and bye, when she was almost in despair, the little girl came upon two trees that promised to furnish her with plenty of food

One was quite full of square paper boxes, which grew in clusters on all the limbs, and upon the biggest and ripest boxes the word "Lunch" could be read, in neat raised letters. This tree seemed to bear all the year around, for there were lunch-box blossoms on some of the branches, and on others tiny little lunch-boxes that were as yet quite green, and evidently not fit to eat until they had grown bigger.

The leaves of this tree were all paper napkins, and it presented a very pleasing appearance to the hungry little girl.

But the tree next to the lunch-box tree was even more wonderful, for it bore quantities of tin dinner-pails, which were so full and heavy that the stout

branches bent underneath their weight. Some were
small and dark-brown in color; those larger were
of a dull tin color; but the really ripe ones were
pails of bright tin that shone and glistened beautifully in the rays of sunshine that touched them.

Dorothy was delighted, and even the yellow hen
acknowledged that she was surprised.

The little girl stood on tip-toe and picked one
of the nicest and biggest lunch-boxes, and then she
sat down upon the ground and eagerly opened it.
Inside she found, nicely wrapped in white papers, a
ham sandwich, a piece of sponge-cake, a pickle, a
slice of new cheese and an apple. Each thing had
a separate stem, and so had to be picked off the side
of the box; but Dorothy found them all to be delicious, and she ate every bit of luncheon in the box
before she had finished.

"A lunch isn't zactly breakfast," she said to Billina, who sat beside her curiously watching. "But
when one is hungry one can eat even supper in the
morning, and not complain."

"I hope your lunch-box was perfectly ripe," observed the yellow hen, in a anxious tone. "So much
sickness is caused by eating green things."

"Oh, I'm sure it was ripe," declared Dorothy,
"all, that is, 'cept the pickle, and a pickle just *has*

THE LITTLE GIRL PICKED ONE OF THE LUNCH-BOXES

to be green, Billina. But everything tasted perfectly splendid, and I'd rather have it than a church picnic. And now I think I'll pick a dinner-pail, to have when I get hungry again, and then we'll start out and 'splore the country, and see where we are."

"Havn't you any idea what country this is?" inquired Billina.

"None at all. But listen: I'm quite sure it's a fairy country, or such things as lunch-boxes and dinner-pails wouldn't be growing upon trees. Besides, Billina, being a hen, you wouldn't be able to talk in any civ'lized country, like Kansas, where no fairies live at all."

"Perhaps we're in the Land of Oz," said the hen, thoughtfully.

"No, that can't be," answered the little girl; because I've been to the Land of Oz, and it's all surrounded by a horrid desert that no one can cross."

"Then how did you get away from there again?" asked Billina.

"I had a pair of silver shoes, that carried me through the air; but I lost them," said Dorothy.

"Ah, indeed," remarked the yellow hen, in a tone of unbelief.

"Anyhow," resumed the girl, "there is no sea-

The Letters in the Sand

shore near the Land of Oz, so this must surely be some other fairy country."

"While she was speaking she selected a bright and pretty dinner-pail that seemed to have a stout handle, and picked it from its branch. Then, accompanied by the yellow hen, she walked out of the shadow of the trees toward the sea-shore.

They were part way across the sands when Billina suddenly cried, in a voice of terror:

"What's that?"

Dorothy turned quickly around, and saw coming out of a path that led from between the trees the most peculiar person her eyes had ever beheld.

It had the form of a man, except that it walked, or rather rolled, upon all fours, and its legs were the same length as its arms, giving them the appearance of the four legs of a beast. Yet it was no beast that Dorothy had discovered, for the person was clothed most gorgeously in embroidered garments of many colors, and wore a straw hat perched jauntily upon the side of its head. But it differed from human beings in this respect, that instead of hands and feet there grew at the end of its arms and legs round wheels, and by means of these wheels it rolled very swiftly over the level ground. Afterward Dorothy found that these odd wheels were of the same hard substance that our finger-nails and toe-nails are composed of, and she also learned that creatures of this strange race were born in this queer fashion. But when our little girl first caught sight of the first individual of a race that was destined to cause her a lot of trouble, she had an idea that the brilliantly-clothed personage was on roller-skates, which were attached to his hands as well as to his feet.

"Run!" screamed the yellow hen, fluttering away in great fright. "It's a Wheeler!"

"IT'S A WHEELER!"

"A Wheeler?" exclaimed Dorothy. "What can that be?"

"Don't you remember the warning in the sand: 'Beware the Wheelers'? Run, I tell you—run!"

So Dorothy ran, and the Wheeler gave a sharp, wild cry and came after her in full chase.

Looking over her shoulder as she ran, the girl now saw a great procession of Wheelers emerging from the forest—dozens and dozens of them—all clad in splendid, tight-fitting garments and all rolling swiftly toward her and uttering their wild, strange cries.

"They're sure to catch us!" panted the girl, who was still carrying the heavy dinner-pail she had picked. "I can't run much farther, Billina."

"Climb up this hill,—quick!" said the hen; and Dorothy found she was very near to the heap of loose and jagged rocks they had passed on their way to the forest. The yellow hen was even now fluttering among the rocks, and Dorothy followed as best she could, half climbing and half tumbling up the rough and rugged steep.

She was none too soon, for the foremost Wheeler reached the hill a moment after her; but while the girl scrambled up the rocks the creature stopped short with howls of rage and disappointment.

46

The Letters in the Sand

Dorothy now heard the yellow hen laughing, in her cackling, henny way.

"Don't hurry, my dear," cried Billina. "They can't follow us among these rocks, so we're safe enough now."

Dorothy stopped at once and sat down upon a broad boulder, for she was all out of breath.

The rest of the Wheelers had now reached the foot of the hill, but it was evident that their wheels would not roll upon the rough and jagged rocks, and therefore they were helpless to follow Dorothy and the hen to where they had taken refuge. But they circled all around the little hill, so the child and Billina were fast prisoners and could not come down without being captured.

Then the creatures shook their front wheels at Dorothy in a threatening manner, and it seemed they were able to speak as well as to make their dreadful outcries, for several of them shouted:

"We'll get you in time, never fear! And when we do get you, we'll tear you into little bits!"

"Why are you so cruel to me?" asked Dorothy. "I'm a stranger in your country, and have done you no harm."

"No harm!" cried one who seemed to be their leader. "Did you not pick our lunch-boxes and dinner-pails? Have you not a stolen dinner-pail still in your hand?"

"I only picked one of each," she answered. "I was hungry, and I didn't know the trees were yours."

"That is no excuse," retorted the leader, who was clothed in a most gorgeous suit. "It is the law here that whoever picks a dinner-pail without our permission must die immediately."

"Don't you believe him," said Billina. "I'm sure the trees do not belong to these awful creatures. They are fit for any mischief, and it's my opinion they would try to kill us just the same if you hadn't picked a dinner-pail."

"I think so, too," agreed Dorothy. "But what shall we do now?"

"Stay where we are," advised the yellow hen. "We are safe from the Wheelers until we starve to death, anyhow; and before that time comes a good many things can happen."

Tiktok *the* Machine Man

After an hour or so most of
the band of Wheelers
rolled back into the forest,
leaving only three of their
number to guard the hill.
These curled themselves up like
big dogs and pretended to go to
sleep on the sands; but neither Dorothy nor Billina were fooled by this
trick, so they remained in security
among the rocks and paid no attention
to their cunning enemies.

Finally the hen, fluttering over the mound,
exclaimed: "Why, here's a path!"

So Dorothy at once clambered to where Billina sat, and there, sure enough, was a smooth path

49

cut between the rocks. It seemed to wind around the mound from top to bottom, like a cork-screw, twisting here and there between the rough boulders but always remaining level and easy to walk upon.

Indeed, Dorothy wondered at first why the Wheelers did not roll up this path; but when she followed it to the foot of the mound she found that several big pieces of rock had been placed directly across the end of the way, thus preventing any one outside from seeing it and also preventing the Wheelers from using it to climb up the mound.

Then Dorothy walked back up the path, and followed it until she came to the very top of the hill, where a solitary round rock stood that was bigger than any of the others surrounding it. The path came to an end just beside this great rock, and for a moment it puzzled the girl to know why the path had been made at all. But the hen, who had been gravely following her around and was now perched upon a point of rock behind Dorothy, suddenly remarked:

"It looks something like a door, doesn't it?"

"What looks like a door?" enquired the child.

"Why, that crack in the rock, just facing you," replied Billina, whose little round eyes were very sharp and seemed to see everything. "It runs up

one side and down the other, and across the top and the bottom."

"What does?"

"Why, the crack. So I think it must be a door of rock, although I do not see any hinges."

"Oh, yes," said Dorothy, now observing for the first time the crack in the rock. "And isn't this a key-hole, Billina?" pointing to a round, deep hole at one side of the door.

"Of course. If we only had the key, now, we

could unlock it and see what is there," replied the yellow hen. "May be it's a treasure chamber full of diamonds and rubies, or heaps of shining gold, or——"

"That reminds me," said Dorothy, "of the golden key I picked up on the shore. Do you think that it would fit this key-hole, Billina?"

"Try it and see," suggested the hen.

So Dorothy searched in the pocket of her dress and found the golden key. And when she had put it into the hole of the rock, and turned it, a sudden sharp snap was heard; then, with a solemn creak that made the shivers run down the child's back, the face of the rock fell outward, like a door on hinges, and revealed a small dark chamber just inside.

"Good gracious!" cried Dorothy, shrinking back as far as the narrow path would let her.

For, standing within the narrow chamber of rock, was the form of a man—or, at least, it seemed like a man, in the dim light. He was only about as tall as Dorothy herself, and his body was round as a ball and made out of burnished copper. Also his head and limbs were copper, and these were jointed or hinged to his body in a peculiar way, with metal caps over the joints, like the armor worn by knights in days of old. He stood perfectly still, and where

"THIS COPPER MAN IS NOT ALIVE AT ALL"

the light struck upon his form it glittered as if made of pure gold.

"Don't be frightened," called Billina, from her perch. "It isn't alive."

"I see it isn't," replied the girl, drawing a long breath.

"It is only made out of copper, like the old kettle in the barn-yard at home," continued the hen, turning her head first to one side and then to the other, so that both her little round eyes could examine the object.

"Once," said Dorothy, "I knew a man made out of tin, who was a woodman named Nick Chopper. But he was as alive as we are, 'cause he was born a real man, and got his tin body a little at a time—first a leg and then a finger and then an ear—for the reason that he had so many accidents with his axe, and cut himself up in a very careless manner."

"Oh," said the hen, with a sniff, as if she did not believe the story.

"But this copper man," continued Dorothy, looking at it with big eyes, "is not alive at all, and I wonder what it was made for, and why it was locked up in this queer place."

"That is a mystery," remarked the hen, twisting her head to arrange her wing-feathers with her bill.

Tiktok, The Machine Man

Dorothy stepped inside the little room to get a back view of the copper man, and in this way discovered a printed card that hung between his shoulders, it being suspended from a small copper peg at the back of his neck. She unfastened this card and returned to the path, where the light was better, and sat herself down upon a slab of rock to read the printing.

"What does it say?" asked the hen, curiously.

Dorothy read the card aloud, spelling out the big words with some difficulty; and this is what she read:

SMITH & TINKER'S

Patent Double-Action, Extra-Responsive,
Thought-Creating, Perfect-Talking

MECHANICAL MAN

Fitted with our Special Clock-Work Attachment.

Thinks, Speaks, Acts, and Does Everything but Live.

Manufactured only at our Works at Evna, Land of Ev.
All infringements will be promptly Prosecuted according to Law.

"How queer!" said the yellow hen. "Do you think that is all true, my dear?"

"I don't know," answered Dorothy, who had more to read. "Listen to this, Billina:"

DIRECTIONS FOR USING:

For THINKING:—Wind the Clock-work Man under his left arm, (marked No. 1.)

For SPEAKING:—Wind the Clock-work Man under his right arm, (marked No. 2.)

For WALKING and ACTION:—Wind Clock-work in the middle of his back, (marked No. 3.)

N. B.—This Mechanism is guaranteed to work perfectly for a thousand years.

"Well, I declare!" gasped the yellow hen, in amazement; "if the copper man can do half of these things he is a very wonderful machine. But I suppose it is all humbug, like so many other patented articles."

"We might wind him up," suggested Dorothy, "and see what he'll do."

"Where is the key to the clock-work?" asked Billina.

"Hanging on the peg where I found the card."

"Then," said the hen, "let us try him, and find out if he will go. He is warranted for a thousand years, it seems; but we do not know how long he has been standing inside this rock."

Dorothy had already taken the clock key from the peg.

DOROTHY WOUND UP NUMBER ONE

"Which shall I wind up first?" she asked, looking again at the directions on the card.

"Number One, I should think," returned Billina. "That makes him think, doesn't it?"

"Yes," said Dorothy, and wound up Number One, under the left arm.

"He doesn't seem any different," remarked the hen, critically.

"Why, of course not; he is only thinking, now," said Dorothy.

"I wonder what he is thinking about."

"I'll wind up his talk, and then perhaps he can tell us," said the girl.

So she wound up Number Two, and immediately the clock-work man said, without moving any part of his body except his lips:

"Good morn-ing, lit-tle girl. Good morn-ing, Mrs. Hen."

The words sounded a little hoarse and creakey, and they were uttered all in the same tone, without any change of expression whatever; but both Dorothy and Billina understood them perfectly.

"Good morning, sir," they answered, politely.

"Thank you for res-cu-ing me," continued the machine, in the same monotonous voice, which

Tiktok, The Machine Man

seemed to be worked by a bellows inside of him, like the little toy lambs and cats the children squeeze so that they will make a noise.

"Don't mention it," answered Dorothy. And then, being very curious, she asked: "How did you come to be locked up in this place?"

"It is a long sto-ry," replied the copper man; "but I will tell it to you brief-ly. I was pur-chased from Smith & Tin-ker, my man-u-fac-tur-ers, by a cru-el King of Ev, named Ev-ol-do, who used to beat all his serv-ants un-til they died. How-ev-er, he was not a-ble to kill me, be-cause I was not a-live, and one must first live in or-der to die. So that all his beat-ing did me no harm, and mere-ly kept my cop-per bod-y well pol-ished.

"This cru-el king had a love-ly wife and ten beau-ti-ful chil-dren—five boys and five girls—but in a fit of an-ger he sold them all to the Nome King, who by means of his mag-ic arts changed them all in-to oth-er forms and put them in his un-der-ground pal-ace to or-na-ment the rooms.

"Af-ter-ward the King of Ev re-gret-ted his wick-ed ac-tion, and tried to get his wife and chil-dren a-way from the Nome King, but with-out a-vail. So, in de-spair, he locked me up in this rock, threw the key in-to the o-cean, and then jumped in af-ter it and was drowned."

"How very dreadful!" exclaimed Dorothy.

"It is, in-deed," said the machine. "When I found my-self im-pris-oned I shout-ed for help un-til my voice ran down; and then I walked back and forth in this lit-tle room un-til my ac-tion ran down; and then I stood still and thought un-til my thoughts ran down. Af-ter that I re-mem-ber noth-ing un-til you wound me up a-gain."

"It's a very wonderful story," said Dorothy, "and

THE COPPER MAN WALKED OUT OF THE ROCKY CAVERN

proves that the Land of Ev is really a fairy land, as I thought it was."

"Of course it is," answered the copper man. "I do not sup-pose such a per-fect ma-chine as I am could be made in an-y place but a fair-y land."

"I've never seen one in Kansas," said Dorothy.

"But where did you get the key to un-lock this door?" asked the clock-work voice.

"I found it on the shore, where it was prob'ly washed up by the waves," she answered. "And now, sir, if you don't mind, I'll wind up your action."

"That will please me ve-ry much," said the machine.

So she wound up Number Three, and at once the copper man in a somewhat stiff and jerky fashion walked out of the rocky cavern, took off his copper hat and bowed politely, and then kneeled before Dorothy. Said he:

"From this time forth I am your o-be-di-ent ser-vant. What-ev-er you com-mand, that I **will do** will-ing-ly—if you keep me wound up."

"What is your name?" she asked.

"Tik-tok," he replied. "My for-mer **mas-ter** gave me that name be-cause my clock-work **al-ways** ticks when it is wound up."

"I can hear it now," said the yellow hen.

"So can I," said Dorothy. And then she **added,**

with some anxiety: "You don't strike, do you?"

"No," answered Tiktok; "and there is no a-larm con-nec-ted with my ma-chin-er-y. I can tell the time, though, by speak-ing, and as I nev-er sleep I can wak-en you at an-y hour you wish to get up in the morn-ing."

"That's nice," said the little girl; "only I never wish to get up in the morning."

"You can sleep until I lay my egg," said the yel-low hen. "Then, when I cackle, Tiktok will know it is time to waken you."

"Do you lay your egg very early?" asked Dorothy.

"About eight o'clock," said Billina. "And every-body ought to be up by that time, I'm sure."

Dorothy Opens the Dinner Pail

"Now
Tiktok," said Dorothy,
"the first thing to be done
is to find a way for us to
escape from these rocks. The
Wheelers are down below, you
know, and threaten to kill us."

"There is no rea-son to be a-fraid
of the Wheel-ers," said Tiktok, the
words coming more slowly than before.

"Why not?" she asked.

"Be-cause they are ag-g-g--gr-gr-r-r-"
He gave a sort of gurgle and stopped
short, waving his hands frantically until suddenly he became motionless, with one arm in
the air and the other held stiffly before him with
all the copper fingers of the hand spread out like a fan.

64

Dorothy Opens the Dinner Pail

"Dear me!" said Dorothy, in a frightened tone. "What can the matter be?"

"He's run down, I suppose," said the hen, calmly. "You couldn't have wound him up very tight."

"I didn't know how much to wind him," replied the girl; "but I'll try to do better next time."

She ran around the copper man to take the key from the peg at the back of his neck, but it was not there.

"It's gone!" cried Dorothy, in dismay.

"What's gone?" asked Billina.

"The key."

"It probably fell off when he made that low bow to you," returned the hen. "Look around, and see if you cannot find it again."

Dorothy looked, and the hen helped her, and by and by the girl discovered the clock-key, which had fallen into a crack of the rock.

At once she wound up Tiktok's voice, taking care to give the key as many turns as it would go around. She found this quite a task, as you may imagine if you have ever tried to wind a clock, but the machine man's first words were to assure Dorothy that he would now run for at least twenty-four hours.

"You did not wind me much, at first," he calmly said, "and I told you that long sto-ry a-bout King

Ev-ol-do; so it is no won-der that I ran down."

She next rewound the action clock-work, and then Billina advised her to carry the key to Tiktok in her pocket, so it would not get lost again.

"And now," said Dorothy, when all this was ac-complished, "tell me what you were going to say about the Wheelers."

"Why, they are noth-ing to be fright-en'd at," said the machine. "They try to make folks be-lieve that they are ver-y ter-ri-ble, but as a mat-ter of

Dorothy Opens the Dinner Pail

fact the Wheel-ers are harm-less e-nough to an-y one that dares to fight them. They might try to hurt a lit-tle girl like you, per-haps, be-cause they are ver-y mis-chiev-ous. But if I had a club they would run a-way as soon as they saw me."

"Haven't you a club?" asked Dorothy.

"No," said Tiktok.

"And you won't find such a thing among these rocks, either," declared the yellow hen.

"Then what shall we do?" asked the girl.

"Wind up my think-works tight-ly, and I will try to think of some oth-er plan," said Tiktok.

So Dorothy rewound his thought machinery, and while he was thinking she decided to eat her dinner. Billina was already pecking away at the cracks in the rocks, to find something to eat, so Dorothy sat down and opened her tin dinner-pail.

In the cover she found a small tank that was full of very nice lemonade. It was covered by a cup, which might also, when removed, be used to drink the lemonade from. Within the pail were three slices of turkey, two slices of cold tongue, some lobster salad, four slices of bread and butter, a small custard pie, an orange and nine large strawberries, and some nuts and raisins. Singularly enough, the nuts in this dinner-pail grew already cracked, so that

Dorothy had no trouble in picking out their meats to eat.

She spread the feast upon the rock beside her and began her dinner, first offering some of it to Tiktok, who declined because, as he said, he was merely a machine. Afterward she offered to share with Bil-lina, but the hen murmured something about "dead things" and said she preferred her bugs and ants.

"Do the lunch-box trees and the dinner-pail trees belong to the Wheelers?" the child asked Tiktok, while engaged in eating her meal.

"Of course not," he answered. "They be-long to the roy-al fam-il-y of Ev, on-ly of course there is no roy-al fam-il-y just now be-cause King Ev-ol-do jumped in-to the sea and his wife and ten chil-dren have been trans-formed by the Nome King. So there is no one to rule the Land of Ev, that I can think of. Per-haps it is for this rea-son that the Wheel-ers claim the trees for their own, and pick the lunch-eons and din-ners to eat them-selves. But they be-long to the King, and you will find the roy-al "E" stamped up-on the bot-tom of ev-er-y din-ner pail."

Dorothy turned the pail over, and at once dis-covered the royal mark upon it, as Tiktok had said.

"Are the Wheelers the only folks living in the Land of Ev?" enquired the girl.

DOROTHY OPENED HER TIN DINNER-PAIL

"No; they on-ly in-hab-it a small por-tion of it just back of the woods," replied the machine. "But they have al-ways been mis-chiev-ous and im-per-ti-nent, and my old mas-ter, King Ev-ol-do, used to car-ry a whip with him, when he walked out, to keep the crea-tures in or-der. When I was first made the Wheel-ers tried to run o-ver me, and butt me with their heads; but they soon found I was built of too sol-id a ma-ter-i-al for them to in-jure."

"You seem very durable," said Dorothy. "Who made you?"

"The firm of Smith & Tin-ker, in the town of Ev-na, where the roy-al pal-ace stands," answered Tiktok.

"Did they make many of you?" asked the child.

"No; I am the on-ly au-to-mat-ic me-chan-i-cal man they ev-er com-plet-ed," he replied. "They were ver-y won-der-ful in-ven-tors, were my mak-ers, and quite ar-tis-tic in all they did."

"I am sure of that," said Dorothy. "Do they live in the town of Evna now?"

"They are both gone," replied the machine. "Mr. Smith was an art-ist, as well as an in-vent-or, and he paint-ed a pic-ture of a riv-er which was so nat-ur-al that, as he was reach-ing a-cross it to paint some flow-ers on the op-po-site bank, he fell in-to the wa-ter and was drowned."

70

Dorothy Opens the Dinner Pail

"Oh, I'm sorry for that!" exclaimed the little girl.

"Mis-ter Tin-ker," continued Tiktok, "made a lad-der so tall that he could rest the end of it a-gainst the moon, while he stood on the high-est rung and picked the lit-tle stars to set in the points of the king's crown. But when he got to the moon Mis-ter Tin-ker found it such a love-ly place that he de-cid-ed to live there, so he pulled up the lad-der af-ter him and we have nev-er seen him since."

"He must have been a great loss to this country," said Dorothy, who was bv this time eating her custard pie.

"He was," acknowledged Tiktok. "Also he is a great loss to me. For if I should get out of or-der I do not know of an-y one a-ble to re-pair me, be-cause I am so com-pli-cat-ed. You have no i-de-a how full of ma-chin-er-y I am."

"I can imagine it," said Dorothy, readily.

"And now," continued the machine, "I must stop talk-ing and be-gin think-ing a-gain of a way to es-cape from this rock." So he turned half way around, in order to think without being disturbed.

"The best thinker I ever knew," said Dorothy to the yellow hen, "was a scarecrow."

"Nonsense!" snapped Billina.

"It is true," declared Dorothy. "I met him in

the Land of Oz, and he travelled with me to the city of the great Wizard of Oz, so as to get some brains, for his head was only stuffed with straw. But it seemed to me that he thought just as well before he got his brains as he did afterward."

"Do you expect me to believe all that rubbish about the Land of Oz?" enquired Billina, who seemed a little cross—perhaps because bugs were scarce.

"What rubbish?" asked the child, who was now finishing her nuts and raisins.

"Why, your impossible stories about animals that can talk, and a tin woodman who is alive, and a scarecrow who can think."

"They are all there," said Dorothy, "for I have seen them."

"I don't believe it!" cried the hen, with a toss of her head.

"That's 'cause you're so ign'rant," replid the girl, who was a little offended at her friend Billina's speech.

"In the Land of Oz," remarked Tiktok, turning toward them, "an-y-thing is pos-si-ble. For it is a won-der-ful fair-y coun-try."

"There, Billina! what did I say?" cried Dorothy. And then she turned to the machine and asked in an eager tone: "Do you know the Land of Oz, Tiktok?"

MISTER TINKER VISITS THE MOON

"No; but I have heard a-bout it," said the copper man. "For it is on-ly sep-a-ra-ted from this Land of Ev by a broad des-ert."

Dorothy clapped her hands together delightedly.

"I'm glad of that!" she exclaimed. "It makes me quite happy to be so near my old friends. The scarecrow I told you of, Billina, is the King of the Land of Oz."

"Par-don me. He is not the king now," said Tiktok.

"He was when I left there," declared Dorothy.

"I know," said Tiktok, "but there was a rev-o-lu-tion in the Land of Oz, and the Scare-crow was de-posed by a sol-dier wo-man named Gen-er-al Jin-jur. And then Jin-jur was de-posed by a lit-tle girl named Oz-ma, who was the right-ful heir to the throne and now rules the land un-der the ti-tle of Oz-ma of Oz."

"That is news to me," said Dorothy, thoughtfully. "But I s'pose lots of things have happened since I left the Land of Oz. I wonder what has become of the Scarecrow, and of the Tin Woodman, and the Cowardly Lion. And I wonder who this girl Ozma is, for I never heard of her before."

But Tiktok did not reply to this. He had turned around again to resume his thinking.

Dorothy Opens the Dinner Pail

Dorothy packed the rest of the food back into the pail, so as not to be wasteful of good things, and the yellow hen forgot her dignity far enough to pick up all of the scattered crumbs, which she ate rather greedily, although she had so lately pretended to despise the things that Dorothy preferred as food.

By this time Tiktok approached them with his stiff bow.

"Be kind e-nough to fol-low me," he said, "and I will lead you a-way from here to the town of Ev-na, where you will be more com-for-ta-ble, and al-so I will pro-tect you from the Wheel-ers."

"All right," answered Dorothy, promptly. "I'm ready!"

The Heads of Langwidere

They

walked slowly down the
path between the rocks,
Tiktok going first, Dorothy
following him, and the yellow
hen trotting along last of all.

At the foot of the path the
copper man leaned down and
tossed aside with ease the rocks that
cumbered the way.   Then he turned
to Dorothy and said:

"Let me car-ry your din-ner-pail."

She placed it in his right hand at once,
and the copper fingers closed firmly over the
stout handle.

Then the little procession marched out upon
the level sands.

The Heads of Langwidere

As soon as the three Wheelers who were guarding the mound saw them, they began to shout their wild cries and rolled swiftly toward the little group, as if to capture them or bar their way. But when the foremost had approached near enough, Tiktok swung the tin dinner-pail and struck the Wheeler a sharp blow over its head with the queer weapon. Perhaps it did not hurt very much, but it made a great noise, and the Wheeler uttered a howl and tumbled over upon its side. The next minute it scrambled to its wheels and rolled away as fast as it could go, screeching with fear at the same time.

"I told you they were harm-less," began Tiktok; but before he could say more another Wheeler was upon them. Crack! went the dinner-pail against its head, knocking its straw hat a dozen feet away; and that was enough for this Wheeler, also. It rolled away after the first one, and the third did not wait to be pounded with the pail, but joined its fellows as quickly as its wheels would whirl.

The yellow hen gave a cackle of delight, and flying to a perch upon Tiktok's shoulder, she said:

"Bravely done, my copper friend! and wisely thought of, too. Now we are free from those ugly creatures."

But just then a large band of Wheelers rolled

77

from the forest, and relying upon their numbers to conquer, they advanced fiercely upon Tiktok. Dorothy grabbed Billina in her arms and held her tight, and the machine embraced the form of the little girl with his left arm, the better to protect her. Then the Wheelers were upon them.

Rattlety, bang! bang! went the dinner-pail in every direction, and it made so much clatter bumping against the heads of the Wheelers that they were much more frightened than hurt and fled in a great panic. All, that is, except their leader. This Wheeler had stumbled against another and fallen flat upon his back, and before he could get his wheels under him to rise again, Tiktok had fastened his copper fingers into the neck of the gorgeous jacket of his foe and held him fast.

"Tell your peo-ple to go a-way," commanded the machine.

The leader of the Wheelers hesitated to give this order, so Tiktok shook him as a terrier dog does a rat, until the Wheeler's teeth rattled together with a noise like hailstones on a window pane. Then, as soon as the creature could get its breath, it shouted to the others to roll away, which they immediately did.

"Now," said Tiktok, "you shall come with us and tell me what I want to know."

The Heads of Langwidere

"You'll be sorry for treating me in this way," whined the Wheeler. "I'm a terribly fierce person."

"As for that," answered Tiktok, "I am only a ma-chine, and can-not feel sor-row or joy, no mat-ter what hap-pens. But you are wrong to think your-self ter-ri-ble or fierce."

"Why so?" asked the Wheeler.

"Be-cause no one else thinks as you do. Your wheels make you help-less to in-jure an-y one. For you have no fists and can not scratch or e-ven pull hair. Nor have you an-y feet to kick with. All you can do is to yell and shout, and that does not hurt an-y one at all."

The Wheeler burst into a flood of tears, to Dorothy's great surprise.

"Now I and my people are ruined forever!" he sobbed; "for you have discovered our secret. Being so helpless, our only hope is to make people afraid of us, by pretending we are very fierce and terrible, and writing in the sand warnings to Beware the Wheelers. Until now we have frightened everyone, but since you have discovered our weakness our enemies will fall upon us and make us very miserable and unhappy."

"Oh, no," exclaimed Dorothy, who was sorry to see this beautifully dressed Wheeler so miserable; "Tiktok will keep your secret, and so will Billina and I. Only, you must promise not to try to frighten children any more, if they come near to you."

"I won't—indeed I won't!" promised the Wheeler, ceasing to cry and becoming more cheerful. "I'm not really bad, you know; but we have to pretend to be terrible in order to prevent others from attacking us."

"That is not ex-act-ly true," said Tiktok, starting to walk toward the path through the forest, and

ON THE WAY TO THE ROYAL PALACE OF EV

still holding fast to his prisoner, who rolled slowly along beside him. "You and your peo-ple are full of mis-chief, and like to both-er those who fear you. And you are of-ten im-pu-dent and dis-a-gree-a-ble, too. But if you will try to cure those faults I will not tell any-one how help-less you are."

"I'll try, of course," replied the Wheeler, eagerly. "And thank you, Mr. Tiktok, for your kindness."

"I am on-ly a ma-chine," said Tiktok. "I can not be kind an-y more than I can be sor-ry or glad. I can on-ly do what I am wound up to do."

"Are you wound up to keep my secret?" asked the Wheeler, anxiously.

"Yes; if you be-have your-self. But tell me: who rules the Land of Ev now?" asked the machine.

"There is no ruler," was the answer, "because every member of the royal family is imprisoned by the Nome King. But the Princess Langwidere, who is a niece of our late King Evoldo, lives in a part of the royal palace and takes as much money out of the royal treasury as she can spend. The Princess Langwidere is not exactly a ruler, you see, because she doesn't rule; but she is the nearest approach to a ruler we have at present."

"I do not re-mem-ber her," said Tiktok. "What does she look like?"

The Heads of Langwidere

"That I cannot say," replied the Wheeler, "although I have seen her twenty times. For the Princess Langwidere is a different person every time I see her, and the only way her subjects can recognize her at all is by means of a beautiful ruby key which she always wears on a chain attached to her left wrist. When we see the key we know we are beholding the Princess."

"That is strange," said Dorothy, in astonishment. "Do you mean to say that so many different princesses are one and the same person?"

"Not exactly," answered the Wheeler. "There is, of course, but one princess; but she appears to us in many forms, which are all more or less beautiful."

"She must be a witch," exclaimed the girl.

"I do not think so," declared the Wheeler. "But there is some mystery connected with her, nevertheless. She is a very vain creature, and lives mostly in a room surrounded by mirrors, so that she can admire herself whichever way she looks."

No one answered this speech, because they had just passed out of the forest and their attention was fixed upon the scene before them—a beautiful vale in which were many fruit trees and green fields, with pretty farm-houses scattered here and there and broad, smooth roads that led in every direction.

In the center of this lovely vale, about a mile from where our friends were standing, rose the tall spires of the royal palace, which glittered brightly against their background of blue sky. The palace was surrounded by charming grounds, full of flowers and shrubbery. Several tinkling fountains could be seen, and there were pleasant walks bordered by rows of white marble statuary.

All these details Dorothy was, of course, unable to notice or admire until they had advanced along the road to a position quite near to the palace, and she was still looking at the pretty sights when her little party entered the grounds and approached the big front door of the king's own apartments. To their disappointment they found the door tightly closed. A sign was tacked to the panel which read as follows:

OWNER ABSENT.

Please Knock at the Third Door in the Left Wing.

"Now," said Tiktok to the captive Wheeler, "you must show us the way to the Left Wing."

A SIGN WAS TACKED TO THE PANEL

"Very well," agreed the prisoner, "it is around here at the right."

"How can the left wing be at the right?" demanded Dorothy, who feared the Wheeler was fooling them.

"Because there used to be three wings, and two were torn down, so the one on the right is the only one left. It is a trick of the Princess Langwidere to prevent visitors from annoying her."

Then the captive led them around to the wing, after which the machine man, having no further use for the Wheeler, permitted him to depart and rejoin his fellows. He immediately rolled away at a great pace and was soon lost to sight.

Tiktok now counted the doors in the wing and knocked loudly upon the third one.

It was opened by a little maid in a cap trimmed with gay ribbons, who bowed respectfully and asked:

"What do you wish, good people?"

"Are you the Princess Langwidere?" asked Dorothy.

"No, miss; I am her servant," replied the maid.

"May I see the Princess, please?"

"I will tell her you are here, miss, and ask her to grant you an audience," said the maid. "Step in, please, and take a seat in the drawing-room."

The Heads of Langwidere

So Dorothy walked in, followed closely by the machine. But as the yellow hen tried to enter after them, the little maid cried "Shoo!" and flapped her apron in Billina's face.

"Shoo, yourself!" retorted the hen, drawing back in anger and ruffling up her feathers. "Haven't you any better manners than that?"

"Oh, do you talk?" enquired the maid, evidently surprised.

"Can't you hear me?" snapped Billina. "Drop

that apron, and get out of the doorway, so that I may enter with my friends!"

"The Princess won't like it," said the maid, hesitating.

"I don't care whether she likes it or not," replied Billina, and fluttering her wings with a loud noise she flew straight at the maid's face. The little servant at once ducked her head, and the hen reached Dorothy's side in safety.

"Very well," sighed the maid; "if you are all ruined because of this obstinate hen, don't blame me for it. It isn't safe to annoy the Princess Langwidere."

"Tell her we are waiting, if you please," Dorothy requested, with dignity. "Billina is my friend, and must go wherever I go."

Without more words the maid led them to a richly furnished drawing-room, lighted with subdued rainbow tints that came in through beautiful stained-glass windows.

"Remain here," she said. "What names shall I give the Princess?"

"I am Dorothy Gale, of Kansas," replied the child; "and this gentleman is a machine named Tiktok, and the yellow hen is my friend Billina."

The little servant bowed and withdrew, going

"THE PRINCESS WON'T LIKE IT," SAID THE MAID

through several passages and mounting two marble stairways before she came to the apartments occupied by her mistress.

Princess Langwidere's sitting-room was panelled with great mirrors, which reached from the ceiling to the floor; also the ceiling was composed of mirrors, and the floor was of polished silver that reflected every object upon it. So when Langwidere sat in her easy chair and played soft melodies upon her mandolin, her form was mirrored hundreds of times, in walls and ceiling and floor, and whichever way the lady turned her head she could see and admire her own features. This she loved to do, and just as the maid entered she was saying to herself:

"This head with the auburn hair and hazel eyes is quite attractive. I must wear it more often than I have done of late, although it may not be the best of my collection."

"You have company, Your Highness," announced the maid, bowing low.

"Who is it?" asked Langwidere, yawning.

"Dorothy Gale of Kansas, Mr. Tiktok and Billina," answered the maid.

"What a queer lot of names!" murmured the Princess, beginning to be a little interested. "What are they like? Is Dorothy Gale of Kansas pretty?

The Heads of Langwidere

"She might be called so," the maid replied.

"And is Mr. Tiktok attractive?" continued the Princess.

"That I cannot say, Your Highness. But he seems very bright. Will Your Gracious Highness see them?"

"Oh, I may as well, Nanda. But I am tired admiring this head, and if my visitor has any claim to beauty I must take care that she does not surpass me. So I will go to my cabinet and change to No. 17, which I think is my best appearance. Don't you?"

"Your No. 17 is exceedingly beautiful," answered Nanda, with another bow.

Again the Princess yawned. Then she said:

"Help me to rise."

So the maid assisted her to gain her feet, although Langwidere was the stronger of the two; and then the Princess slowly walked across the silver floor to her cabinet, leaning heavily at every step upon Nanda's arm.

Now I must explain to you that the Princess Langwidere had thirty heads—as many as there are days in the month. But of course she could only wear one of them at a time, because she had but one neck. These heads were kept in what she called her "cabinet," which was a beautiful dressing-room that lay just between Langwidere's sleeping-chamber and the mirrored sitting-room. Each head was in a separate cupboard lined with velvet. The cupboards ran all around the sides of the dressing-room, and had elaborately carved doors with gold numbers on the outside and jewelled-framed mirrors on the inside of them.

When the Princess got out of her crystal bed in the morning she went to her cabinet, opened one of the velvet-lined cupboards, and took the head it contained from its golden shelf. Then, by the aid of the mirror inside the open door, she put on the head—as neat and straight as could be—and afterward called her maids to robe her for the day. She always wore a simple white costume, that suited all the heads. For, being able to change her face whenever she liked, the Princess had no interest in wearing a variety of gowns, as have other ladies who are compelled to wear the same face constantly.

Of course the thirty heads were in great variety, no two formed alike but all being of exceeding loveliness. There were heads with golden hair, brown hair, rich auburn hair and black hair; but none with gray hair. The heads had eyes of blue, of gray, of hazel, of brown and of black; but there were no red eyes among them, and all were bright

BY THE AID OF THE MIRROR SHE PUT ON THE HEAD

and handsome. The noses were Grecian, Roman, retroussé and Oriental, representing all types of beauty; and the mouths were of assorted sizes and shapes, displaying pearly teeth when the heads smiled. As for dimples, they appeared in cheeks and chins, wherever they might be most charming, and one or two heads had freckles upon the faces to contrast the better with the brilliancy of their complexions.

One key unlocked all the velvet cupboards containing these treasures—a curious key carved from a single blood-red ruby—and this was fastened to a strong but slender chain which the Princess wore around her left wrist.

When Nanda had supported Langwidere to a position in front of cupboard No. 17, the Princess unlocked the door with her ruby key and after handing head No. 9, which she had been wearing, to the maid, she took No. 17 from its shelf and fitted it to her neck. It had black hair and dark eyes and a lovely pearl-and-white eomplexion, and when Langwidere wore it she knew she was remarkably beautiful in appearance.

There was only one trouble with No. 17; the temper that went with it (and which was hidden somewhere under the glossy black hair) was fiery, harsh and haughty in the extreme, and it often led the Princess to do unpleasant things which she regretted when she came to wear her other heads.

But she did not remember this today, and went to meet her guests in the drawing-room with a feeling of certainty that she would surprise them with her beauty.

However, she was greatly disappointed to find that her visitors were merely a small girl in a gingham dress, a copper man that would only go when wound up, and a yellow hen that was sitting contentedly in Langwidere's best work-basket, where there was a china egg used for darning stockings.*

"Oh!" said Langwidere, slightly lifting the nose of No. 17. "I thought some one of importance had called."

"Then you were right," declared Dorothy. "I'm a good deal of 'portance myself, and when Billina lays an egg she has the proudest cackle you ever heard. As for Tiktok, he's the——"

"Stop——Stop!" commanded the Princess, with an angry flash of her splendid eyes. "How dare you annoy me with your senseless chatter?"

---

*It may surprise you to learn that a princess ever does such a common thing as darn stockings. But, if you will stop to think, you will realize that a princess is sure to wear holes in her stockings, the same as other people; only it isn't considered quite polite to mention the matter.

"Why, you horrid thing!" said Dorothy, who was not accustomed to being treated so rudely.

The Princess looked at her more closely.

"Tell me," she resumed, "are you of royal blood?"

"Better than that, ma'am," said Dorothy. "I came from Kansas."

"Huh!" cried the Princess, scornfully. "You are a foolish child, and I cannot allow you to annoy me. Run away, you little goose, and bother some one else."

Dorothy was so indignant that for a moment she could find no words to reply. But she rose from her chair, and was about to leave the room when the Princess, who had been scanning the girl's face, stopped her by saying, more gently:

"Come nearer to me."

Dorothy obeyed, without a thought of fear, and stood before the Princess while Langwidere examined her face with careful attention.

"You are rather attractive," said the lady, presently. "Not at all beautiful, you understand, but you have a certain style of prettiness that is different from that of any of my thirty heads. So I believe I'll take your head and give you No. 26 for it."

"Well, I b'lieve you won't!" exclaimed Dorothy.

"It will do you no good to refuse," continued the

"WELL I B'LIEVE YOU WON'T!" EXCLAIMED DOROTHY

Princess; "for I need your head for my collection,
and in the Land of Ev my will is law. I never have
cared much for No. 26, and you will find that it is
very little worn. Besides, it will do you just as well
as the one you're wearing, for all practical purposes."

"I don't know anything about your No. 26, and
I don't want to," said Dorothy, firmly. "I'm not
used to taking cast-off things, so I'll just keep my
own head."

"You refuse?" cried the Princess, with a frown.

"Of course I do," was the reply.

"Then," said Langwidere, "I shall lock you up
in a tower until you decide to obey me. Nanda,"
turning to her maid, "call my army."

Nanda rang a silver bell, and at once a big fat
colonel in a bright red uniform entered the room,
followed by ten lean soldiers, who all looked sad
and discouraged and saluted the princess in a very
melancholy fashion.

"Carry that girl to the North Tower and lock
her up!" cried the Princess, pointing to Dorothy.

"To hear is to obey," answered the big red colonel,
and caught the child by her arm. But at that moment Tiktok raised his dinner-pail and pounded it
so forcibly against the colonel's head that the big
officer sat down upon the floor with a sudden bump,

looking both dazed and very much astonished.

"Help!" he shouted, and the ten lean soldiers sprang to assist their leader.

There was great excitement for the next few moments, and Tiktok had knocked down seven of the army, who were sprawling in every direction upon the carpet, when suddenly the machine paused, with the dinner-pail raised for another blow, and remained perfectly motionless.

"My ac-tion has run down," he called to Dorothy. "Wind me up, quick."

She tried to obey, but the big colonel had by this time managed to get upon his feet again, so he grabbed fast hold of the girl and she was helpless to escape.

"This is too bad," said the machine. "I ought to have run six hours lon-ger, at least, but I sup-pose my long walk and my fight with the Wheel-ers made me run down fast-er than us-u-al."

"Well, it can't be helped," said Dorothy, with a sigh.

"Will you exchange heads with me?" demanded the Princess.

"No, indeed!" cried Dorothy.

"Then lock her up," said Langwidere to her soldiers, and they led Dorothy to a high tower at the north of the palace and locked her securely within.

The soldiers afterward tried to lift Tiktok, but they found the machine so solid and heavy that they could not stir it. So they left him standing in the center of the drawing-room.

"People will think I have a new statue," said Langwidere, "so it won't matter in the least, and Nanda can keep him well polished."

"What shall we do with the hen?" asked the colonel, who had just discovered Billina in the work-basket.

"Put her in the chicken-house," answered the Princess. "Some day I'll have her fried for breakfast."

"She looks rather tough, Your Highness," said Nanda, doubtfully.

"That is a base slander!" cried Billina, struggling frantically in the colonel's arms. "But the breed of chickens I come from is said to be poison to all princesses."

"Then," remarked Langwidere, "I will not fry the hen, but keep her to lay eggs; and if she doesn't do her duty I'll have her drowned in the horse trough."

Ozma of Oz to the Rescue

Nanda

brought Dorothy bread
and water for her supper,
and she slept upon a hard
stone couch with a single
pillow and a silken coverlet.

In the morning she leaned
out of the window of her prison
in the tower to see if there was any
way to escape. The room was not so
very high up, when compared with our
modern buildings, but it was far enough
above the trees and farm houses to give
her a good view of the surrounding country.

To the east she saw the forest, with the sands
beyond it and the ocean beyond that. There
was even a dark speck upon the shore that she

thought might be the chicken-coop in which she had
arrived at this singular country.

Then she looked to the north, and saw a deep
but narrow valley lying between two rocky mountains, and a third mountain that shut off the valley
at the further end.

Westward the fertile Land of Ev suddenly ended
a little way from the palace, and the girl could see
miles and miles of sandy desert that stretched further than her eyes could reach. It was this desert,
she thought, with much interest, that alone separated
her from the wonderful Land of Oz, and she remembered sorrowfully that she had been told no
one had ever been able to cross this dangerous waste
but herself. Once a cyclone had carried her across
it, and a magical pair of silver shoes had carried her
back again. But now she had neither a cyclone nor
silver shoes to assist her, and her condition was sad
indeed. For she had become the prisoner of a dis-
agreeable princess who insisted that she must exchange her head for another one that she was not
used to, and which might not fit her at all.

Really, there seemed no hope of help for her from
her old friends in the Land of Oz. Thoughtfully
she gazed from her narrow window. On all the
desert not a living thing was stirring.

Ozma to the Rescue

Wait, though! Something surely *was* stirring on the desert—something her eyes had not observed at first. Now it seemed like a cloud; now it seemed like a spot of silver; now it seemed to be a mass of rainbow colors that moved swiftly toward her.

What *could* it be, she wondered?

Then, gradually, but in a brief space of time nevertheless, the vision drew near enough to Dorothy to make out what it was.

A broad green carpet was unrolling itself upon the desert, while advancing across the carpet was a wonderful procession that made the girl open her eyes in amazement as she gazed.

First came a magnificent golden chariot, drawn by a great Lion and an immense Tiger, who stood shoulder to shoulder and trotted along as gracefully as a well-matched team of thoroughbred horses. And standing upright within the chariot was a beautiful girl clothed in flowing robes of silver gauze and wearing a jeweled diadem upon her dainty head. She held in one hand the satin ribbons that guided her astonishing team, and in the other an ivory wand that separated at the top into two prongs, the prongs being tipped by the letters "O" and "Z", made of glistening diamonds set closely together.

The girl seemed neither older nor larger than

Dorothy herself, and at once the prisoner in the tower guessed that the lovely driver of the chariot must be that Ozma of Oz of whom she had so lately heard from Tiktok.

Following close behind the chariot Dorothy saw her old friend the Scarecrow, riding calmly astride a wooden Saw-Horse, which pranced and trotted as naturally as any meat horse could have done.

And then came Nick Chopper, the Tin Woodman, with his funnel-shaped cap tipped carelessly over his left ear, his gleaming axe over his right shoulder, and his whole body sparkling as brightly as it had ever done in the old days when first she knew him.

The Tin Woodman was on foot, marching at the head of a company of twenty-seven soldiers, of whom some were lean and some fat, some short and some tall; but all the twenty-seven were dressed in handsome uniforms of various designs and colors, no two being alike in any respect.

Behind the soldiers the green carpet rolled itself up again, so that there was always just enough of it for the procession to walk upon, in order that their feet might not come in contact with the deadly, life-destroying sands of the desert.

Dorothy knew at once it was a magic carpet she

THE MAGIC CARPET

beheld, and her heart beat high with hope and joy as she realized she was soon to be rescued and allowed to greet her dearly beloved friends of Oz— the Scarecrow, the Tin Woodman and the Cowardly Lion.

Indeed, the girl felt herself as good as rescued as soon as she recognized those in the procession, for she well knew the courage and loyalty of her old comrades, and also believed that any others who came from their marvelous country would prove to be pleasant and reliable acquaintances.

As soon as the last bit of desert was passed and all the procession, from the beautiful and dainty Ozma to the last soldier, had reached the grassy meadows of the Land of Ev, the magic carpet rolled itself together and entirely disappeared.

Then the chariot driver turned her Lion and Tiger into a broad roadway leading up to the palace, and the others followed, while Dorothy still gazed from her tower window in eager excitement.

They came quite close to the front door of the palace and then halted, the Scarecrow dismounting from his Saw-Horse to approach the sign fastened to the door, that he might read what it said.

Dorothy, just above him, could keep silent no longer.

Ozma to the Rescue

"Here I am!" she shouted, as loudly as she could. "Here's Dorothy!"

"Dorothy who?" asked the Scarecrow, tipping his head to look upward until he nearly lost his balance and tumbled over backward.

"Dorothy Gale, of course. Your friend from Kansas," she answered.

"Why, hello, Dorothy!" said the Scarecrow. "What in the world are you doing up there?"

"Nothing," she called down, "because there's nothing to do. Save me, my friend—save me!"

"You seem to be quite safe now," replied the Scarecrow.

"But I'm a prisoner. I'm locked in, so that I can't get out," she pleaded.

"That's all right," said the Scarecrow. "You might be worse off, little Dorothy. Just consider the matter. You can't get drowned, or be run over by a Wheeler, or fall out of an apple-tree. Some folks would think they were lucky to be up there."

"Well, I don't," declared the girl, "and I want to get down immed'i'tly and see you and the Tin Woodman and the Cowardly Lion."

"Very well," said the Scarecrow, nodding. "It shall be just as you say, little friend. Who locked you up?"

"The princess Langwidere, who is a horrid creature," she answered.

At this Ozma, who had been listening carefully to the conversation, called to Dorothy from her chariot, asking:

"Why did the Princess lock you up, my dear?"

"Because," exclaimed Dorothy, "I wouldn't let her have my head for her collection, and take an old, cast-off head in exchange for it."

"SAVE ME, MY FRIEND—SAVE ME!"

"I do not blame you," exclaimed Ozma, promptly. "I will see the Princess at once, and oblige her to liberate you."

"Oh, thank you very, very much!" cried Dorothy, who as soon as she heard the sweet voice of the girlish Ruler of Oz knew that she would soon learn to love her dearly.

Ozma now drove her chariot around to the third door of the wing, upon which the Tin Woodman boldly proceeded to knock.

As soon as the maid opened the door Ozma, bearing in her hand her ivory wand, stepped into the hall and made her way at once to the drawing-room, followed by all her company, except the Lion and the Tiger. And the twenty-seven soldiers made such a noise and a clatter that the little maid Nanda ran away screaming to her mistress, whereupon the Princess Langwidere, roused to great anger by this rude invasion of her palace, came running into the drawing room without any assistance whatever.

There she stood before the slight and delicate form of the little girl from Oz and cried out;—

"How dare you enter my palace unbidden? Leave this room at once, or I will bind you and all your people in chains, and throw you into my darkest dungeons!"

"What a dangerous lady!" murmured the Scarecrow, in a soft voice.

"She seems a little nervous," replied the Tin Woodman.

But Ozma only smiled at the angry Princess.

"Sit down, please," she said, quietly. "I have traveled a long way to see you, and you must listen to what I have to say."

"Must!" screamed the Princess, her black eyes flashing with fury—for she still wore her No. 17 head. "Must, to *me*!"

"To be sure," said Ozma. "I am Ruler of the Land of Oz, and I am powerful enough to destroy all your kingdom, if I so wish. Yet I did not come here to do harm, but rather to free the royal family of Ev from the thrall of the Noma King, the news having reached me that he is holding the Queen and her children prisoners."

Hearing these words, Langwidere suddenly became quiet.

"I wish you could, indeed, free my aunt and her ten royal children," said she, eagerly. "For if they were restored to their proper forms and station they could rule the Kingdom of Ev themselves, and that would save me a lot of worry and trouble. At present there are at least ten minutes every day that I must devote to affairs of state, and I would like to be able to spend my whole time in admiring my beautiful heads."

"Then we will presently discuss this matter," said Ozma, "and try to find a way to liberate your aunt and cousins. But first you must liberate another prisoner—the little girl you have locked up in your tower."

"Of course," said Langwidere, readily. "I had forgotten all about her. That was yesterday, you know, and a Princess cannot be expected to

"WHAT A DANGEROUS LADY!" MURMURED THE SCARECROW

remember today what she did yesterday. Come with me, and I will release the prisoner at once."

So Ozma followed her, and they passed up the stairs that led to the room in the tower.

While they were gone Ozma's followers remained in the drawing-room, and the Scarecrow was leaning against a form that he had mistaken for a copper statue when a harsh, metallic voice said suddenly in his ear:

"Get off my foot, please. You are scratch-ing my pol-ish."

"Oh, excuse me!" he replied, hastily drawing back. "Are you alive?"

"No," said Tiktok, "I am on-ly a ma-chine. But I can think and speak and act, when I am pro-per-ly wound up. Just now my ac-tion is run down, and Dor-o-thy has the key to it."

"That's all right," replied the Scarecrow. Dorothy will soon be free, and then she'll attend to your works. But it must be a great misfortune not to be alive. I'm sorry for you."

"Why?" asked Tiktok.

"Because you have no brains, as I have," said the Scarecrow.

"Oh, yes, I have," returned Tiktok. "I am fit-ted with Smith & Tin-ker's Improved Com-bina-tion Steel Brains. They are what make me think. What sort of brains are you fit-ted with?"

"I don't know," admitted the Scarecrow. "They were given to me by the great Wizard of Oz, and I didn't get a chance to examine them before he put them in. But they work splendidly and my conscience is very active. Have you a con-science?"

"No," said Tiktok.

"And no heart, I suppose?" added the Tin Wood-man, who had been listening with interest to this conversation.

"No," said Tiktok.

"Then," continued the Tin Woodman, "I regret to say that you are greatly inferior to my friend the Scarecrow, and to myself. For we are both alive, and he has brains which do not need to be wound up, while I have an excellent heart that is continu-ally beating in my bosom."

"I con-grat-u-late you," replied Tiktok. "I can-not help be-ing your in-fer-i-or for I am a mere ma-chine. When I am wound up I do my du-ty by go-ing just as my ma-chin-er-y is made to go. You have no i-de-a how full of ma-chin-er-y I am."

"I can guess," said the Scarecrow, looking at the machine man curiously. "Some day I'd like to take you apart and see just how you are made."

"Do not do that, I beg of you," said Tiktok; "for you could not put me to-geth-er a-gain, and my use-ful-ness would be de-stroyed."

"Oh! are you useful?" asked the Scarecrow, surprised.

"Ve-ry," said Tiktok.

"In that case," the Scarecrow kindly promised, "I won't fool with your interior at all. For I am a poor mechanic, and might mix you up."

"Thank you," said Tiktok.

Just then Ozma re-entered the room, leading Dorothy by the hand and followed closely by the Princess Langwidere.

The Hungry Tiger

The first thing Dorothy did was to rush into the embrace of the Scarecrow, whose painted face beamed with delight as he pressed her form to his straw-padded bosom. Then the Tin Woodman embraced her—very gently, for he knew his tin arms might hurt her if he squeezed too roughly.

These greetings having been exchanged, Dorothy took the key to Tiktok from her pocket and wound up the machine man's action, so that he could bow properly when introduced to the rest of the company.

While doing this she told them now useful Tiktok
had been to her, and both the Scarecrow and the
Tin Woodman shook hands with the machine once
more and thanked him for protecting their friend.

Then Dorothy asked: "Where is Billina?"

"I don't know," said the Scarecrow. "Who is
Billina?"

"She's a yellow hen who is another friend of
mine," answered the girl, anxiously. "I wonder
what has become of her?"

"She is in the chicken house, in the back yard,"
said the Princess. "My drawing-room is no place
for hens."

Without waiting to hear more Dorothy ran to
get Billina, and just outside the door she came upon
the Cowardly Lion, still hitched to the chariot beside the great Tiger. The Cowardly Lion had a
big bow of blue ribbon fastened to the long hair
between his ears, and the Tiger wore a bow of red
ribbon on his tail, just in front of the bushy end.

In an instant Dorothy was hugging the huge Lion
joyfully.

"I'm *so* glad to see you again!" she cried.

"I am also glad to see you, Dorothy," said the
Lion. "We've had some fine adventures together,
haven't we?"

"Yes, indeed," she replied. "How are you?"

"As cowardly as ever," the beast answered in a meek voice. "Every little thing scares me and makes my heart beat fast. But let me introduce to you a new friend of mine, the Hungry Tiger."

"Oh! Are you hungry?" she asked, turning to the other beast, who was just then yawning so widely that he displayed two rows of terrible teeth and a mouth big enough to startle anyone.

"Dreadfully hungry," answered the Tiger, snapping his jaws together with a fierce click.

"Then why don't you eat something?" she asked.

"It's no use," said the Tiger sadly. "I've tried that, but I always get hungry again."

"Why, it is the same with me," said Dorothy. "Yet I keep on eating."

"But you eat harmless things, so it doesn't matter," replied the Tiger. "For my part, I'm a savage beast, and have an appetite for all sorts of poor little living creatures, from a chipmonk to fat babies.

"How dreadful!" said Dorothy.

"Isn't it, though?" returned the Hungry Tiger, licking his lips with his long red tongue. "Fat babies! Don't they sound delicious? But I've never eaten any, because my conscience tells me it is wrong. If I had no conscience I would probably eat the babies and then get hungry again, which would mean that I had sacrificed the poor babies for nothing. No; hungry I was born, and hungry I shall die. But I'll not have any cruel deeds on my conscience to be sorry for."

"I think you are a very good tiger," said Dorothy, patting the huge head of the beast.

"In that you are mistaken," was the reply. "I am a good beast, perhaps, but a disgracefully bad tiger. For it is the nature of tigers to be cruel and ferocious, and in refusing to eat harmless living creatures I am acting as no good tiger has ever

THE HUNGRY TIGER

before acted. That is why I left the forest and joined my friend the Cowardly Lion."

"But the Lion is not really cowardly," said Dorothy. "I have seen him act as bravely as can be."

"All a mistake, my dear," protested the Lion gravely. "To others I may have seemed brave, at times, but I have never been in any danger that I was not afraid."

"Nor I," said Dorothy, truthfully   "But I must go and set free Billina, and then I will see you again."

She ran around to the back yard of the palace and soon found the chicken house, being guided to it by a loud cackling and crowing and a distracting hubbub of sounds such as chickens make when they are excited.

Something seemed to be wrong in the chicken house, and when Dorothy looked through the slats in the door she saw a group of hens and roosters huddled in one corner and watching what appeared to be a whirling ball of feathers. It bounded here and there about the chicken house, and at first Dorothy could not tell what it was, while the screeching of the chickens nearly deafened her.

But suddenly the bunch of feathers stopped whirling, and then, to her amazement, the girl saw

The Hungry Tiger

Billina crouching upon the prostrate form of a speckled rooster. For an instant they both remained motionless, and then the yellow hen shook her wings to settle the feathers and walked toward the door with a strut of proud defiance and a cluck of victory, while the speckled rooster limped away to the group of other chickens, trailing his crumpled plumage in the dust as he went.

"Why, Billina!" cried Dorothy, in a shocked voice; "have you been fighting?"

"I really think I have," retorted Billina. "Do you think I'd let that speckled villain of a rooster lord it over *me*, and claim to run this chicken house, as long as I'm able to peck and scratch? Not if my name is Bill!"

"It isn't Bill, it's Billina; and you're talking slang, which is very undig'n'fied," said Dorothy, reprovingly. "Come here, Billina, and I'll let you out; for Ozma of Oz is here, and has set us free."

So the yellow hen came to the door, which Dorothy unlatched for her to pass through, and the other chickens silently watched them from their corner without offering to approach nearer.

The girl lifted her friend in her arms and exclaimed:

"Oh, Billina! how dreadful you look. You've

lost a lot of feathers, and one of your eyes is nearly pecked out, and your comb is bleeding!"

"That's nothing," said Billina. "Just look at the speckled rooster! Didn't I do him up brown?"

Dorothy shook her head.

"I don't 'prove of this, at all," she said, carrying Billina away toward the palace. "It isn't a good thing for you to 'sociate with those common chickens. They would soon spoil your good manners, and you wouldn't be respec'able any more."

"I didn't ask to associate with them," replied Billina. "It is that cross old Princess who is to blame. But I was raised in the United States, and I won't allow any one-horse chicken of the Land of Ev to run over me and put on airs, as long as I can lift a claw in self-defense."

"Very well, Billina," said Dorothy. "We won't talk about it any more."

Soon they came to the Cowardly Lion and the Hungry Tiger to whom the girl introduced the Yellow Hen.

"Glad to meet any friend of Dorothy's," said the Lion, politely. "To judge by your present appearance, you are not a coward, as I am."

"Your present appearance makes my mouth water," said the Tiger, looking at Billina greedily.

"WHY, BILLINA!" CRIED DOROTHY; "HAVE YOU BEEN FIGHTING?"

"My, my! how good you would taste if I could only crunch you between my jaws. But don't worry. You would only appease my appetite for a moment; so it isn't worth while to eat you."

"Thank you," said the hen, nestling closer in Dorothy's arms.

"Besides, it wouldn't be right," continued the Tiger, looking steadily at Billina and clicking his jaws together.

"Of course not," cried Dorothy, hastily. "Billina is my friend, and you mustn't ever eat her under any circ'mstances."

"I'll try to remember that," said the Tiger; "but I'm a little absent-minded, at times."

Then Dorothy carried her pet into the drawing-room of the palace, where Tiktok, being invited to do so by Ozma, had seated himself between the Scarecrow and the Tin Woodman. Opposite to them sat Ozma herself and the Princess Langwidere, and beside them there was a vacant chair for Dorothy.

Around this important group was ranged the Army of Oz, and as Dorothy looked at the handsome uniforms of the Twenty-Seven she said:

"Why, they seem to be all officers."

"They are, all except one," answered the Tin Woodman. "I have in my Army eight Generals,

six Colonels, seven Majors and five Captains, besides
one private for them to command. I'd like to promote the private, for I believe no private should ever
be in public life; and I've also noticed that officers
usually fight better and are more reliable than common soldiers. Besides, the officers are more important looking, and lend dignity to our army."

"No doubt you are right," said Dorothy, seating
herself beside Ozma.

"And now," announced the girlish Ruler of Oz,
"we will hold a solemn conference to decide the
best manner of liberating the royal family of this
fair Land of Ev from their long imprisonment."

The Royal Family *of* Ev

The

Tin Woodman was the first to address the meeting.

"To begin with," said he, "word came to our noble and illustrous Ruler, Ozma of Oz, that the wife and ten children—five boys and five girls—of the former King of Ev, by name Evoldo, have been enslaved by the Nome King and are held prisoners in his underground palace. Also that there was no one in Ev powerful enough to release them. Naturally our Ozma wished to undertake the adventure of liberating the poor prisoners; but for a long time she could find no way to cross the great

The Royal Family of Ev

desert between the two countries. Finally she went to a friendly sorceress of our land named Glinda the Good, who heard the story and at once presented Ozma a magic carpet, which would continually unroll beneath our feet and so make a comfortable path for us to cross the desert. As soon as she had received the carpet our gracious Ruler ordered me to assemble our army, which I did. You behold in these bold warriors the pick of all the finest soldiers of Oz; and, if we are obliged to fight the Nome King, every officer as well as the private, will battle fiercely unto death."

Then Tiktok spoke.

"Why should you fight the Nome King?" he asked. "He has done no wrong."

"No wrong!" cried Dorothy. "Isn't it wrong to imprison a queen mother and her ten children?"

"They were sold to the Nome King by King Ev-ol-do," replied Tiktok. "It was the King of Ev who did wrong, and when he re-al-ized what he had done he jumped in-to the sea and drowned him-self."

"This is news to me," said Ozma, thoughtfully. "I had supposed the Nome King was all to blame in the matter. But, in any case, he must be made to liberate the prisoners."

"My uncle Evoldo was a very wicked man,"

declared the Princess Langwidere. "If he had drowned himself before he sold his family, no one would have cared. But he sold them to the powerful Nome King in exchange for a long life, and afterward destroyed the life by jumping into the sea."

"Then," said Ozma, "he did not get the long life, and the Nome King must give up the prisoners. Where are they confined?"

"No one knows, exactly," replied the Princess. "For the king, whose name is Roquat of the Rocks, owns a splendid palace underneath the great mountain which is at the north end of this kingdom, and he has transformed the queen and her children into ornaments and bric-a-brac with which to decorate his rooms."

"I'd like to know," said Dorothy, "who this Nome King is?"

"I will tell you," replied Ozma. "He is said to be the Ruler of the Underground World, and commands the rocks and all that the rocks contain. Under his rule are many thousands of the Nomes, who are queerly shaped but powerful sprites that labor at the furnaces and forges of their king, making gold and silver and other metals which they conceal in the crevices of the rocks, so that those living upon the earth's surface can only find them with great dfficulty. Also they make diamonds and rubies and emeralds, which they hide in the ground; so that the kingdom of the Nomes is wonderfully rich, and all we have of precious stones and silver and gold is what we take from the earth and rocks where the Nome King has hidden them."

"I understand," said Dorothy, nodding her little head wisely.

"For the reason that we often steal his treasures," continued Ozma, "the Ruler of the Underground World is not fond of those who live upon the earth's surface, and never appears among us. If we wish to see King Roquat of the Rocks, we must visit his own country, where he is all powerful, and therefore it will be a dangerous undertaking."

"But, for the sake of the poor prisoners," said Dorothy, "we ought to do it."

"We shall do it," replied the Scarecrow, "although it requires a lot of courage for me to go near to the furnaces of the Nome King. For I am only stuffed with straw, and a single spark of fire might destroy me entirely."

"The furnaces may also melt my tin," said the Tin Woodman; "but I am going."

"I can't bear heat," remarked the Princess Langwidere, yawning lazily, "so I shall stay at home. But I wish you may have success in your undertaking, for I am heartily tired of ruling this stupid kingdom, and I need more leisure in which to admire my beautiful heads."

"We do not need you," said Ozma. "For, if with the aid of my brave followers I cannot accomplish my purpose, then it would be useless for you to undertake the journey."

"Quite true," sighed the Princess. "So, if you'll excuse me, I will now retire to my cabinet. I've worn this head quite awhile, and I want to change it for another."

When she had left them (and you may be sure no one was sorry to see her go) Ozma said to Tiktok:

"Will you join our party?"

"I am the slave of the girl Dor-oth-y, who rescued me from pris-on," replied the machine. "Where she goes I will go."

"Oh, I am going with my friends, of course," said Dorothy, quickly. "I wouldn't miss the fun for anything. Will you go, too, Billina?"

"To be sure," said Billina in a careless tone. She was smoothing down the feathers of her back and not paying much attention.

"I CAN'T BEAR HEAT," REMARKED LANGWIDERE

"Heat is just in her line," remarked the Scarecrow. "If she is nicely roasted, she will be better than ever."

"Then" said Ozma, "we will arrange to start for the Kingdom of the Nomes at daybreak tomorrow. And, in the meantime, we will rest and prepare ourselves for the journey."

Although Princess Langwidere did not again appear to her guests, the palace servants waited upon the strangers from Oz and did everything in their power to make the party comfortable. There were many vacant rooms at their disposal, and the brave Army of twenty-seven was easily provided for and liberally feasted.

The Cowardly Lion and the Hungry Tiger were unharnessed from the chariot and allowed to roam at will throughout the palace, where they nearly frightened the servants into fits, although they did no harm at all. At one time Dorothy found the little maid Nanda crouching in terror in a corner, with the Hungry Tiger standing before her.

"You certainly look delicious," the beast was saying. "Will you kindly give me permission to eat you?"

"No, no, no!" cried the maid in reply.

"Then," said the Tiger, yawning frightfully,

The Royal Family of Ev

"please to get me about thirty pounds of tenderloin steak, cooked rare, with a peck of boiled potatoes on the side, and five gallons of ice-cream for dessert."

"I—I'll do the best I can!" said Nanda, and she ran away as fast as she could go.

"Are you so very hungry?" asked Dorothy, in wonder.

"You can hardly imagine the size of my appetite," replied the Tiger, sadly. "It seems to fill my whole body, from the end of my throat to the tip of my tail. I am very sure the appetite doesn't fit me, and is too large for the size of my body. Some day, when I meet a dentist with a pair of forceps, I'm going to have it pulled."

"What, your tooth?" asked Dorothy.

"No, my appetite," said the Hungry Tiger.

The little girl spent most of the afternoon talking with the Scarecrow and the Tin Woodman, who related to her all that had taken place in the Land of Oz since Dorothy had left it. She was much interested in the story of Ozma, who had been, when a baby, stolen by a wicked old witch and transformed into a boy. She did not know that she had ever been a girl until she was restored to her natural form by a kind sorceress. Then it was found that she was the only child of

DOROTHY RELATED TO THEM HER OWN ADVENTURES

The Royal Family of Ev

the former Ruler of Oz, and was entitled to rule in his place. Ozma had many adventures, however, before she regained her father's throne, and in these she was accompanied by a pumpkin-headed man, a highly magnified and thoroughly educated Woggle-Bug, and a wonderful sawhorse that had been brought to life by means of a magic powder. The Scarecrow and the Tin Woodman had also assisted her; but the Cowardly Lion, who ruled the great forest as the King of Beasts, knew nothing of Ozma until after she became the reigning princess of Oz. Then he journeyed to the Emerald City to see her, and on hearing she was about to visit the Land of Ev to set free the royal family of that country, the Cowardly Lion begged to go with her, and brought along his friend, the Hungry Tiger, as well.

Having heard this story, Dorothy related to them her own adventures, and then went out with her friends to find the Sawhorse, which Ozma had caused to be shod with plates of gold, so that its legs would not wear out.

They came upon the Sawhorse standing motionless beside the garden gate, but when Dorothy was introduced to him he bowed politely and blinked his eyes, which were knots of wood, and wagged his tail, which was only the branch of a tree.

"What a remarkable thing, to be alive!" exclaimed Dorothy.

"I quiet agree with you," replied the Sawhorse, in a rough but not unpleasant voice. "A creature like me has no business to live, as we all know. But

it was the magic powder that did it, so I cannot justly be blamed."

"Of course not," said Dorothy. "And you seem to be of some use, 'cause I noticed the Scarecrow riding upon your back."

"Oh, yes; I'm of use," returned the Sawhorse;

"and I never tire, never have to be fed, or cared for in any way."

"Are you intel'gent?" asked the girl.

"Not very," said the creature. It would be foolish to waste intelligence on a common Sawhorse, when so many professors need it. But I know enough to obey my masters, and to gid-dup, or whoa, when I'm told to. So I'm pretty well satisfied."

That night Dorothy slept in a pleasant little bed-chamber next to that occupied by Ozma of Oz, and Billina perched upon the foot of the bed and tucked her head under her wing and slept as soundly in that position as did Dorothy upon her soft cushions.

But before daybreak every one was awake and stirring, and soon the adventurers were eating a hasty breakfast in the great dining-room of the palace. Ozma sat at the head of a long table, on a raised platform, with Dorothy on her right hand and the Scarecrow on her left. The Scarecrow did not eat, of course; but Ozma placed him near her so that she might ask his advice about the journey while she ate.

Lower down the table were the twenty-seven warriors of Oz, and at the end of the room the Lion and the Tiger were eating out of a kettle that had been placed upon the floor, while Billina fluttered around to pick up any scraps that might be scattered.

It did not take long to finish the meal, and then the Lion and the Tiger were harnessed to the chariot and the party was ready to start for the Nome King's Palace.

First rode Ozma, with Dorothy beside her in the golden chariot and holding Billina fast in her arms. Then came the Scarecrow on the Sawhorse, with the Tin Woodman and Tiktok marching side by side just behind him. After these tramped the Army, looking brave and handsome in their splendid uniforms. The generals commanded the colonels and the colonels commanded the majors and the majors commanded the captains and the captains commanded the private, who marched with an air of proud importance because it required so many officers to give him his orders.

And so the magnificent procession left the palace and started along the road just as day was breaking, and by the time the sun came out they had made good progress toward the valley that led to the Nome King's domain.

The Giant with the Hammer

The road led for a time through a pretty farm country, and then past a picnic grove that was very inviting. But the procession continued to steadily advance until Billina cried in an abrupt and commanding manner:

"Wait—wait!"

Ozma stopped her chariot so suddenly that the Scarecrow's Sawhorse nearly ran into it, and the ranks of the army tumbled over one another before they could come to a halt. Immediately the yellow hen struggled from Dorothy's arms and flew into a clump of bushes by the roadside.

"What's the matter?" called the Tin Woodman, anxiously.

"Why, Billina wants to lay her egg, that's all," said Dorothy.

"Lay her egg!" repeated the Tin Woodman, in astonishment.

"Yes; she lays one every morning, about this time; and it's quite fresh," said the girl.

"But does your foolish old hen suppose that this entire cavalcade, which is bound on an important adventure, is going to stand still while she lays her egg?" enquired the Tin Woodman, earnestly.

"What else can we do?" asked the girl. "It's a habit of Billina's and she can't break herself of it."

"Then she must hurry up," said the Tin Woodman, impatiently.

"No, no!" exclaimed the Scarecrow. "If she hurries she may lay scrambled eggs."

"That's nonsense," said Dorothy. "But Billina won't be long, I'm sure."

So they stood and waited, although all were restless and anxious to proceed. And by and by the yellow hen came from the bushes saying:

"Kut-kut, kut, ka-daw-kutt!" Kut, kut, kut—ka-daw-kut!"

The Giant With the Hammer

"What is she doing—singing her lay?" asked the Scarecrow.

"For-ward—march!" shouted the Tin Woodman, waving his axe, and the procession started just as Dorothy had once more grabbed Billina in her arms.

"Isn't anyone going to get my egg?" cried the hen, in great excitement.

"I'll get it," said the Scarecrow; and at his command the Sawhorse pranced into the bushes. The straw man soon found the egg, which he placed in his jacket pocket. The cavalcade, having moved rapidly on, was even then far in advance; but it did not take the Sawhorse long to catch up with it, and presently the Scarecrow was riding in his accustomed place behind Ozma's chariot.

"What shall I do with the egg?" he asked Dorothy.

"I do not know," the girl answered. "Perhaps the Hungry Tiger would like it."

"It would not be enough to fill one of my back teeth," remarked the Tiger. "A bushel of them, hard boiled, might take a little of the edge off my appetite; but one egg isn't good for anything at all, that I know of."

The Giant With the Hammer

"No; it wouldn't even make a sponge cake," said the Scarecrow, thoughtfully. "The Tin Woodman might carry it with his axe and hatch it; but after all I may as well keep it myself for a souvenir." So he left it in his pocket.

They had now reached that part of the valley that lay between the two high mountains which

Dorothy had seen from her tower window. At the far end was the third great mountain, which blocked the valley and was the northern edge of the Land of Ev. It was underneath this mountain that the Nome King's palace was said to be; but it would

be some time before they reached that place.

The path was becoming rocky and difficult for the wheels of the chariot to pass over, and presently a deep gulf appeared at their feet which was too wide for them to leap. So Ozma took a small square of green cloth from her pocket and threw it upon the ground. At once it became the magic carpet, and unrolled itself far enough for all the cavalcade to walk upon. The chariot now advanced, and the green carpet unrolled before it, crossing the gulf on a level with its banks, so that all passed over in safety.

"That's easy enough," said the Scarecrow. "I wonder what will happen next."

He was not long in making the discovery, for the sides of the mountain came closer together until finally there was but a narrow path between them, along which Ozma and her party were forced to pass in single file

They now heard a low and deep "thump!—thump!—thump!" which echoed throughout the valley and seemed to grow louder as they advanced. Then, turning a corner of rock, they saw before them a huge form, which towered above the path for more than a hundred feet. The form was that of a gigantic man built out of plates of cast iron,

The Giant With the Hammer

and it stood with one foot on either side of the narrow road and swung over its right shoulder an immense iron mallet, with which it constantly pounded the earth. These resounding blows explained the thumping sounds they had heard, for the mallet was much bigger than a barrel, and where it struck the path between the rocky sides of the mountain it filled all the space through which our travelers would be obliged to pass.

Of course they at once halted, a safe distance away from the terrible iron mallet. The magic carpet would do them no good in this case, for it was only meant to protect them from any dangers upon the ground beneath their feet, and not from dangers that appeared in the air above them.

"Wow!" said the Cowardly Lion, with a shudder. "It makes me dreadfully nervous to see that big hammer pounding so near my head. One blow would crush me into a door-mat."

"The ir-on gi-ant is a fine fel-low," said Tiktok, "and works as stead-i-ly as a clock. He was made for the Nome King by Smith & Tin-ker, who made me, and his du-ty is to keep folks from find-ing the un-der-ground pal-ace. Is he not a great work of art?"

"Can he think, and speak, as you do?" asked

Ozma, regarding the giant with wondering eyes.

"No," replied the machine; "he is on-ly made to pound the road, and has no think-ing or speak-ing at-tach-ment. But he pounds ve-ry well, I think."

"Too well," observed the Scarecrow. "He is keeping us from going farther. Is there no way to stop his machinery?"

"On-ly the Nome King, who has the key, can do that," answered Tiktok.

"Then," said Dorothy, anxiously, "what shall we do?"

"Excuse me for a few minutes," said the Scarecrow, "and I will think it over."

He retired, then, to a position in the rear, where he turned his painted face to the rocks and began to think.

Meantime the giant continued to raise his iron mallet high in the air and to strike the path terrific blows that echoed through the mountains like the roar of a cannon. Each time the mallet lifted, however, there was a moment when the path beneath the monster was free, and perhaps the Scarecrow had noticed this, for when he came back to the others he said:

"The matter is a very simple one, after all. We have but to run under the hammer, one at a time,

THE TIGER WENT NEXT

when it is lifted, and pass to the other side before it falls again."

"It will require quick work, if we escape the blow," said the Tin Woodman, with a shake of his head. "But it really seems the only thing to be done. Who will make the first attempt?"

They looked at one another hesitatingly for a moment. Then the Cowardly Lion, who was trembling like a leaf in the wind, said to them:

"I suppose the head of the procession must go first—and that's me. But I'm terribly afraid of the big hammer!"

"What will become of me?" asked Ozma. "You might rush under the hammer yourself, but the chariot would surely be crushed."

"We must leave the chariot," said the Scarecrow. "But you two girls can ride upon the backs of the Lion and the Tiger."

So this was decided upon, and Ozma, as soon as the Lion was unfastened from the chariot, at once mounted the beast's back and said she was ready.

"Cling fast to his mane," advised Dorothy. "I used to ride him myself, and that's the way I held on."

So Ozma clung fast to the mane, and the lion crouched in the path and eyed the swinging mallet

The Giant With the Hammer

carefully until he knew just the instant it would begin to rise in the air.

"Then, before anyone thought he was ready, he made a sudden leap straight between the iron giant's legs, and before the mallet struck the ground again the Lion and Ozma were safe on the other side.

The Tiger went next. Dorothy sat upon his back and locked her arms around his striped neck, for he had no mane to cling to. He made the leap straight and true as an arrow from a bow, and ere Dorothy realized it she was out of danger and standing by Ozma's side.

Now came the Scarecrow on the Sawhorse, and while they made the dash in safety they were within a hair's breadth of being caught by the descending hammer.

Tiktok walked up to the very edge of the spot the hammer struck, and as it was raised for the next blow he calmly stepped forward and escaped its descent. That was an idea for the Tin Woodman to follow, and he also crossed in safety while the great hammer was in the air. But when it came to the twenty-six officers and the private, their knees were so weak that they could not walk a step.

"In battle we are wonderfully courageous," said one of the generals, "and our foes find us very terrible to face. But war is one thing and this is another. When it comes to being pounded upon the head by an iron hammer, and smashed into pancakes, we naturally object."

"Make a run for it," urged the Scarecrow.

"Our knees shake so that we cannot run," answered a captain. "If we should try it we would all certainly be pounded to a jelly."

"Well, well," sighed the Cowardly Lion, "I see, friend Tiger, that we must place ourselves in great danger to rescue this bold army. Come with me, and we will do the best we can."

So, Ozma and Dorothy having already dismounted from their backs, the Lion and the Tiger leaped back again under the awful hammer and returned with two generals clinging to their necks. They repeated this daring passage twelve times, when all the officers had been carried beneath the giant's legs and landed safely on the further side. By that time the beasts were very tired, and panted so hard that their tongues hung out of their great mouths.

"But what is to become of the private?" asked Ozma.

"Oh, leave him there to guard the chariot," said the Lion. "I'm tired out, and won't pass under that mallet again."

THE WOODEN HORSE WAS CARELESS

The officers at once protested that they must have the private with them, else there would be no one for them to command. But neither the Lion or the Tiger would go after him, and so the Scarecrow sent the Sawhorse.

Either the wooden horse was careless, or it failed to properly time the descent of the hammer, for the mighty weapon caught it squarely upon its head, and thumped it against the ground so powerfully that the private flew off its back high into the air, and landed upon one of the giant's cast-iron arms. Here he clung desperately while the arm rose and fell with each one of the rapid strokes.

The Scarecrow dashed in to rescue his Sawhorse, and had his left foot smashed by the hammer before he could pull the creature out of danger. They then found that the Sawhorse had been badly dazed by the blow; for while the hard wooden knot of which his head was formed could not be crushed by the hammer, both his ears were broken off and he would be unable to hear a sound until some new ones were made for him. Also his left knee was cracked, and had to be bound up with a string.

Billina having fluttered under the hammer, it now remained only to rescue the private who was riding upon the iron giant's arm, high in the air.

The Giant With the Hammer

The Scarecrow lay flat upon the ground and called to the man to jump down upon his body, which was soft because it was stuffed with straw. This the private managed to do, waiting until a time when he was nearest the ground and then letting himself drop upon the Scarecrow. He accomplished the feat without breaking any bones, and the Scarecrow declared he was not injured in the least.

Therefore, the Tin Woodman having by this time fitted new ears to the Sawhorse, the entire party proceeded upon its way, leaving the giant to pound the path behind them.

The Nome King

By and by, when they drew near to the mountain that blocked their path and which was the furthermost edge of the Kingdom of Ev, the way grew dark and gloomy for the reason that the high peaks on either side shut out the sunshine. And it was very silent, too, as there were no birds to sing or squirrels to chatter, the trees being left far behind them and only the bare rocks remaining.

Ozma and Dorothy were a little awed by the silence, and all the others were quiet and grave except the Sawhorse, which, as it trotted along with the Scarecrow upon his back, hummed a queer song, of which this was the chorus:

"Would a wooden horse in a woodland go?
Aye, aye! I sigh, he would, although
Had he not had a wooden head
He'd mount the mountain top instead."

But no one paid any attention to this because they were now close to the Nome King's dominions, and his splendid underground palace could not be very far away.

Suddenly they heard a shout of jeering laughter, and stopped short. They would have to stop in a minute, anyway, for the huge mountain barred their further progress and the path ran close up to a wall of rock and ended.

"Who was that laughing?" asked Ozma.

There was no reply, but in the gloom they could see strange forms flit across the face of the rock. Whatever the creations might be they seemed very like the rock itself, for they were the color of rocks and their shapes were as rough and rugged as if they had been broken away from the side of the mountain. They kept close to the steep cliff facing our friends, and glided up and down, and this way and that, with a lack of regularity that was quite confusing. And they seemed not to need places to rest their feet, but clung to the surface of the rock as a fly does to a window-pane, and were never still for a moment.

"Do not mind them," said Tiktok, as Dorothy shrank back. "They are on-ly the Nomes."

"And what are Nomes?" asked the girl, half frightened.

"They are rock fair-ies, and serve the Nome King," replied the machine. "But they will do us no harm. You must call for the King, be-cause with-out him you can ne-ver find the en-trance to the pal-ace."

"*You* call," said Dorothy to Ozma.

Just then the Nomes laughed again, and the sound was so wierd and disheartening that the twenty-six officers commanded the private to "right-about-face!" and they all started to run as fast as they could.

The Tin Woodman at once pursued his army and cried "halt!" and when they had stopped their flight he asked: "Where are you going?"

"I—I find I've forgotten the brush for my whiskers," said a general, trembling with fear. "S-s-so we are g-going back after it!"

"That is impossible," replied the Tin Woodman. "For the giant with the hammer would kill you all if you tried to pass him."

"Oh! I'd forgotten the giant," said the general, turning pale.

"You seem to forget a good many things," remarked the Tin Woodman. "I hope you won't forget that you are brave men."

"Never!" cried the general, slapping his gold-embroidered chest.

"Never!" cried all the other officers, indignantly slapping their chests.

"For my part," said the private, meekly, "I must obey my officers; so when I am told to run, I run; and when I am told to fight, I fight."

"That is right," agreed the Tin Woodman. "And now you must all come back to Ozma, and obey *her* orders. And if you try to run away again I will have her reduce all the twenty-six officers to privates, and make the private your general."

This terrible threat so frightened them that they at once returned to where Ozma was standing beside the Cowardly Lion.

Then Ozma cried out in a loud voice:

"I demand that the Nome King appear to us!"

There was no reply, except that the shifting Nomes upon the mountain laughed in derision.

"You must not command the Nome King," said Tiktok, "for you do not rule him, as you do your own peo-ple."

So Ozma called again, saying:

159

ONLY THE MOCKING LAUGHTER REPLIED TO HER

The Nome King

"I request the Nome King to appear to us."

Only the mocking laughter replied to her, and the shadowy Nomes continued to flit here and there upon the rocky cliff.

"Try en-treat-y," said Tiktok to Ozma. "If he will not come at your re-quest, then the Nome King may list-en to your plead-ing."

Ozma looked around her proudly.

"Do you wish your ruler to plead with this wicked Nome King?" she asked. "Shall Ozma of Oz humble herself to a creature who lives in an underground kingdom?"

"No!" they all shouted, with big voices; and the Scarecrow added:

"If he will not come, we will dig him out of his hole, like a fox, and conquer his stubbornness. But our sweet little ruler must always maintain her dignity, just as I maintain mine."

"I'm not afraid to plead with him," said Dorothy. "I'm only a little girl from Kansas, and we've got more dignity at home than we know what to do with. *I'll* call the Nome King."

"Do," said the Hungry Tiger; "and if he makes hash of you I'll willingly eat you for breakfast to-morrow morning."

So Dorothy stepped forward and said:

161

"*Please* Mr. Nome King, come here and see us."

The Nomes started to laugh again; but a low growl came from the mountain, and in a flash they had all vanished from sight and were silent.

Then a door in the rock opened, and a voice cried:

"Enter!"

"Isn't it a trick?" asked the Tin Woodman.

"Never mind," replied Ozma. "We came here to rescue the poor Queen of Ev and her ten children, and we must run some risks to do so."

"The Nome King is hon-est and good na-tured,"

said Tiktok. "You can trust him to do what is right."

So Ozma led the way, hand in hand with Dorothy, and they passed through the arched doorway of rock and entered a long passage which was lighted by jewels set in the walls and having lamps behind them. There was no one to escort them, or to show them the way, but all the party pressed through the passage until they came to a round, domed cavern that was grandly furnished.

In the center of this room was a throne carved out of a solid boulder of rock, rude and rugged in shape but glittering with great rubies and diamonds and emeralds on every part of its surface. And upon the throne sat the Nome King.

This important monarch of the Underground World was a little fat man clothed in gray-brown garments that were the exact color of the rock throne in which he was seated. His bushy hair and flowing beard were also colored like the rocks, and so was his face. He wore no crown of any sort, and his only ornament was a broad, jewel-studded belt that encircled his fat little body. As for his features, they seemed kindly and good humored, and his eyes were turned merrily upon his visitors as Ozma and Dorothy stood before him with their followers ranged in close order behind them.

"Why, he looks just like Santa Claus—only he isn't the same color!" whispered Dorothy to her friend; but the Nome King heard the speech, and it made him laugh aloud.

> "'He had a red face and a round little belly
> That shook when he laughed like a bowl full of jelly!'"

quoth the monarch, in a pleasant voice; and they could all see that he really did shake like jelly when he laughed.

Both Ozma and Dorothy were much relieved to find the Nome King so jolly, and a minute later he waved his right hand and the girls each found a cushioned stool at her side.

"Sit down, my dears," said the King, "and tell me why you have come all this way to see me, and what I can do to make you happy."

While they seated themselves the Nome King picked up a pipe, and taking a glowing red coal out of his pocket he placed it in the bowl of the pipe and began puffing out clouds of smoke that curled in rings above his head. Dorothy thought this made the little monarch look more like Santa Claus than ever; but Ozma now began speaking, and every one listened intently to her words.

"Your Majesty," said she, "I am the ruler of the Land of Oz, and I have come here to ask you to release the good Queen of Ev and her ten children, whom you have enchanted and hold as your prisoners."

"Oh, no; you are mistaken about that," replied

the King. "They are not my prisoners, but my slaves, whom I purchased from the King of Ev."

"But that was wrong," said Ozma.

"According to the laws of Ev, the king can do no wrong," answered the monarch, eyeing a ring of smoke he had just blown from his mouth; "so that he had a perfect right to sell his family to me in exchange for a long life."

"You cheated him, though," declared Dorothy; "for the King of Ev did not have a long life. He jumped into the sea and was drowned."

"That was not my fault," said the Nome King, crossing his legs and smiling contentedly. "I gave him the long life, all right; but he destroyed it."

"Then how could it be a long life?" asked Dorothy.

"Easily enough," was the reply. "Now suppose, my dear, that I gave you a pretty doll in exchange for a lock of your hair, and that after you had received the doll you smashed it into pieces and destroyed it. Could you say that I had not given you a pretty doll?"

"No," answered Dorothy.

"And could you, in fairness, ask me to return to you the lock of hair, just because you had smashed the doll?"

"No," said Dorothy, again.

"Of course not," the Nome King returned. "Nor will I give up the Queen and her children because the King of Ev destroyed his long life by jumping into the sea. They belong to me and I shall keep them."

"THEY BELONG TO ME AND I SHALL KEEP THEM"

"But you are treating them cruelly," said Ozma, who was much distressed by the King's refusal.

"In what way?" he asked.

"By making them your slaves," said she.

"Cruelty," remarked the monarch, puffing out wreathes of smoke and watching them float into the air, "is a thing I can't abide. So, as slaves must work hard, and the Queen of Ev and her children were delicate and tender, I transformed them all into articles of ornament and bric-a-brac and scattered them around the various rooms of my palace. Instead of being obliged to labor, they merely decorate my apartments, and I really think I have treated them with great kindness."

"But what a dreadful fate is theirs!" exclaimed Ozma, earnestly. "And the Kingdom of Ev is in great need of its royal family to govern it. If you will liberate them, and restore them to their proper forms, I will give you ten ornaments to replace each one you lose."

The Nome King looked grave.

"Suppose I refuse?" he asked.

"Then," said Ozma, firmly, "I am here with my friends and my army to conquer your kingdom and oblige you to obey my wishes."

The Nome King laughed until he choked; and

he choked until he coughed; and he coughed until his face turned from grayish-brown to bright red. And then he wiped his eyes with a rock-colored handkerchief and grew grave again.

"You are as brave as you are pretty, my dear," he said to Ozma. "But you have little idea of the extent of the task you have undertaken. Come with me for a moment."

He arose and took Ozma's hand, leading her to a little door at one side of the room. This he opened and they stepped out upon a balcony, from whence they obtained a wonderful view of the Underground World.

A vast cave extended for miles and miles under the mountain, and in every direction were furnaces and forges glowing brightly and Nomes hammering upon precious metals or polishing gleaming jewels. All around the walls of the cave were thousands of doors of silver and gold, built into the solid rock, and these extended in rows far away into the distance, as far as Ozma's eyes could follow them.

While the little maid from Oz gazed wonderingly upon this scene the Nome King uttered a shrill whistle, and at once all the silver and gold doors flew open and solid ranks of Nome soldiers marched out from every one. So great were their numbers that they quickly filled the immense underground cavern and forced the busy workmen to abandon their tasks.

Although this tremendous army consisted of rock-colored Nomes, all squat and fat, they were clothed in glittering armor of polished steel, inlaid with beautiful gems. Upon his brow each wore a brilliant electric light, and they bore sharp spears and swords and battle-axes of solid bronze. It was evident they were perfectly trained, for they stood in straight rows, rank after rank, with their weapons held erect and true, as if awaiting but the word of command to level them upon their foes.

"This," said the Nome King, "is but a small part of my army. No ruler upon Earth has ever dared to fight me, and no ruler ever will, for I am too powerful to oppose."

He whistled again, and at once the martial array filed through the silver and gold doorways and disappeared, after which the workmen again resumed their labors at the furnaces.

Then, sad and discouraged, Ozma of Oz turned to her friends, and the Nome King calmly reseated himself on his rock throne.

"It would be foolish for us to fight," the girl said to the Tin Woodman. "For our brave Twenty-

"THIS IS BUT A SMALL PART OF MY ARMY"

Seven would be quickly destroyed. I'm sure I do not know how to act in this emergency.

"Ask the King where his kitchen is," suggested the Tiger. "I'm hungry as a bear."

"I might pounce upon the King and tear him in pieces," remarked the Cowardly Lion.

"Try it," said the monarch, lighting his pipe with another hot coal which he took from his pocket.

The Lion crouched low and tried to spring upon the Nome King; but he hopped only a little way into the air and came down again in the same place, not being able to approach the throne by even an inch.

"It seems to me," said the Scarecrow, thoughtfully, "that our best plan is to wheedle his Majesty into giving up his slaves, since he is too great a magician to oppose."

"This is the most sensible thing any of you have suggested," declared the Nome King. "It is folly to threaten me, but I'm so kind-hearted that I cannot stand coaxing or wheedling. If you really wish to accomplish anything by your journey, my dear, Ozma, you must coax me."

"Very well," said Ozma, more cheerfully. "Let us be friends, and talk this over in a friendly manner."

"To be sure," agreed the King, his eyes twinkling merrily.

"I am very anxious," she continued, "to liberate the Queen of Ev and her children who are now ornaments and bric-a-brac in your Majesty's palace, and to restore them to their people. Tell me, sir, how this may be accomplished."

The king remained thoughtful for a moment, after which he asked:

"Are you willing to take a few chances and risks yourself, in order to set free the people of Ev?"

"Yes, indeed!" answered Ozma, eagerly.

"Then," said the Nome King, "I will make you this offer: You shall go alone and unattended into my palace and examine carefully all that the rooms contain. Then you shall have permission to touch eleven different objects, pronouncing at the time the word 'Ev,' and if any one of them, or more than one, proves to be the transformation of the Queen of Ev or any of her ten children, then they will instantly be restored to their true forms and may leave my palace and my kingdom in your company, without any objection whatever. It is possible for you, in this way, to free the entire eleven; but if you do not guess all the objects correctly, and some of the slaves remain transformed, then each one of your

friends and followers may, in turn, enter the palace
and have the same privileges I grant you."

"Oh, thank you! thank you for this kind offer!"
said Ozma, eagerly.

"I make but one condition," added the Nome
King, his eyes twinkling.

"What is it?" she enquired.

"If none of the eleven objects you touch proves
to be the transformation of any of the royal family
of Ev, then, instead of freeing them, you will yourself become enchanted, and transformed into an
article of bric-a-brac or an ornament.   This is only
fair and just, and is the risk you declared you were
willing to take."

The Eleven Guesses

Hearing this condition imposed
by the Nome King, Ozma
became silent and thoughtful, and all her friends looked
at her uneasily.

"Don't you do it!" exclaimed
Dorothy. "If you guess wrong,
you will be enslaved yourself."

"But I shall have eleven guesses,"
answered Ozma. "Surely I ought to
guess one object in eleven correctly; and,
if I do, I shall rescue one of the royal
family and be safe myself. Then the rest of
you may attempt it, and soon we shall free all
those who are enslaved."

"What if we fail?" enquired the Scarecrow. "I'd

175

look nice as a piece of bric-a-brac, wouldn't I?"

"We must not fail!" cried Ozma, courageously. "Having come all this distance to free these poor people, it would be weak and cowardly in us to abandon the adventure. Therefore I will accept the Nome King's offer, and go at once into the royal palace."

"Come along, then, my dear," said the King, climbing down from his throne with some difficulty, because he was so fat; "I'll show you the way."

He approached a wall of the cave and waved his hand. Instantly an opening appeared, through which Ozma, after a smiling farewell to her friends, boldly passed.

She found herself in a splendid hall that was more beautiful and grand than anything she had ever beheld. The ceilings were composed of great arches that rose far above her head, and all the walls and floors were of polished marble exquisitely tinted in many colors. Thick velvet carpets were on the floor and heavy silken draperies covered the arches leading to the various rooms of the palace. The furniture was made of rare old woods richly carved and covered with delicate satins, and the entire palace was lighted by a mysterious rosy glow that seemed to come from no particular place but flooded

The Eleven Guesses

each apartment with its soft and pleasing radiance.

Ozma passed from one room to another, greatly delighted by all she saw. The lovely palace had no other occupant, for the Nome King had left her at the entrance, which closed behind her, and in all the magnificent rooms there appeared to be no other person.

Upon the mantels, and on many shelves and brackets and tables, were clustered ornaments of every description, seemingly made out of all sorts of metals, glass, china, stones and marbles. There were vases, and figures of men and animals, and graven platters and bowls, and mosaics of precious gems, and many other things. Pictures, too, were on the walls, and the underground palace was quite a museum of rare and curious and costly objects.

After her first hasty examination of the rooms Ozma began to wonder which of all the numerous ornaments they contained were the transformations of the royal family of Ev. There was nothing to guide her, for everything seemed without a spark of life. So she must guess blindly; and for the first time the girl came to realize how dangerous was her task, and how likely she was to lose her own freedom in striving to free others from the bondage of the Nome King. No wonder the cunning

OZMA SHUT HER EYES TIGHTLY AND ADVANCED

monarch laughed good naturedly with his visitors, when he knew how easily they might be entrapped.

But Ozma, having undertaken the venture, would not abandon it. She looked at a silver candelabra that had ten branches, and thought: "This may be the Queen of Ev and her ten children." So she touched it and uttered aloud the word "Ev," as the Nome King had instructed her to do when she guessed. But the candelabra remained as it was before.

Then she wandered into another room and touched a china lamb, thinking it might be one of the children she sought. But again she was unsuccessful. Three guesses; four guesses; five, six, seven, eight, nine and ten she made, and still not one of them was right!

The girl shivered a little and grew pale even under the rosy light; for now but one guess remained, and her own fate depended upon the result.

She resolved not to be hasty, and strolled through all the rooms once more, gazing earnestly upon the various ornaments and trying to decide which she would touch. Finally, in despair, she decided to leave it entirely to chance. She faced the doorway of a room, shut her eyes tightly, and then, thrusting aside the heavy draperies, she advanced blindly with her right arm outstretched before her.

Slowly softly she crept forward until her hand came in contact with an object upon a small round table. She did not know what it was, but in a low voice she pronounced the word "Ev."

The rooms were quite empty of life after that. The Nome King had gained a new ornament. For upon the edge of the table rested a pretty grasshopper, that seemed to have been formed from a single emerald. It was all that remained of Ozma of Oz.

In the throne room just beyond the palace the Nome King suddenly looked up and smiled.

"Next!" he said, in his pleasant voice.

Dorothy, the Scarecrow, and the Tin Woodman, who had been sitting in anxious silence, each gave a start of dismay and stared into one another's eyes.

"Has she failed?" asked Tiktok.

"So it seems," answered the little monarch, cheerfully. "But that is no reason one of you should not succeed. The next may have twelve guesses, instead of eleven, for there are now twelve persons transformed into ornaments. Well, well! Which of you goes next?"

"I'll go," said Dorothy.

"Not so," replied the Tin Woodman. "As commander of Ozma's army, it is my privilege to follow her and attempt her rescue."

"Away you go, then," said the Scarecrow. "But be careful, old friend."

"I will," promised the Tin Woodman; and then he followed the Nome King to the entrance to the palace and the rock closed behind him.

The Nome King Laughs

In a moment the King returned to his throne and relighted his pipe, and the rest of the little band of adventurers settled themselves for another long wait. They were greatly disheartened by the failure of their girl Ruler, and the knowledge that she was now an ornament in the Nome King's palace—a dreadful, creepy place in spite of all its magnificence. Without their little leader they did not know what to do next, and each one, down to the trembling private of the army, began to fear he would soon be more ornamental than useful.

The Nome King Laughs

Suddenly the Nome King began laughing.

"Ha, ha, ha! He, he, he! Ho, ho, ho!"

"What's happened?" asked the Scarecrow.

"Why, your friend, the Tin Woodman, has become the funniest thing you can imagine," replied the King, wiping the tears of merriment from his eyes. "No one would ever believe he could make such an amusing ornament. Next!"

They gazed at each other with sinking hearts. One of the generals began to weep dolefully.

"What are you crying for?" asked the Scarecrow, indignant at such a display of weakness.

"He owed me six weeks back pay," said the general, "and I hate to lose him."

"Then you shall go and find him," declared the Scarecrow.

"Me!" cried the general, greatly alarmed.

"Certainly. It is your duty to follow your commander. March!"

"I won't," said the general. "I'd like to, of course; but I just simply *won't*."

The Scarecrow looked enquiringly at the Nome King.

"Never mind," said the jolly monarch. "If he doesn't care to enter the palace and make his guesses I'll throw him into one of my fiery furnaces."

"I'll go!—of course I'm going," yelled the general, as quick as scat. "Where is the entrance—where is it? Let me go at once!"

So the Nome King escorted him into the palace, and again returned to await the result. What the general did, no one can tell; but it was not long before the King called for the next victim, and a colonel was forced to try his fortune.

Thus, one after another, all of the twenty-six officers filed into the palace and made their guesses—and became ornaments.

Meantime the King ordered refreshments to be served to those waiting, and at his command a rudely shaped Nome entered, bearing a tray. This Nome was not unlike the others that Dorothy had seen, but he wore a heavy gold chain around his neck to show that he was the Chief Steward of the Nome King, and he assumed an air of much importance, and even told his majesty not to eat too much cake late at night, or he would be ill.

Dorothy, however, was hungry, and she was not afraid of being ill; so she ate several cakes and found them good, and also she drank a cup of excellent coffee made of a richly flavored clay, browned in the furnaces and then ground fine, and found it most refreshing and not at all muddy.

The Nome King Laughs

Of all the party which had started upon this adventure, the little Kansas girl was now left alone with the Scarecrow, Tiktok, and the private for counsellors and companions. Of course the Cowardly Lion and the Hungry Tiger were still there, but they, having also eaten some of the cakes, had gone to sleep at one side of the cave, while upon the other side stood the Sawhorse, motionless and silent, as became a mere thing of wood. Billina had quietly walked around and picked up the crumbs of cake which had been scattered, and now, as it was long after bed-time, she tried to find some dark place in which to go to sleep.

Presently the hen espied a hollow underneath the King's rocky throne, and crept into it unnoticed. She could still hear the chattering of those around her, but it was almost dark underneath the throne, so that soon she had fallen fast asleep.

"Next!" called the King, and the private, whose turn it was to enter the fatal palace, shook hands with Dorothy and the Scarecrow and bade them a sorrowful good-bye, and passed through the rocky portal.

They waited a long time, for the private was in no hurry to become an ornament and made his guesses very slowly. The Nome King, who seemed to know, by some magical power, all that took place in his beautiful rooms of his palace, grew impatient finally and declared he would sit up no longer.

"I love ornaments," said he, "but I can wait until tomorrow to get more of them; so, as soon as that stupid private is transformed, we will all go to bed and leave the job to be finished in the morning."

"Is it so very late?" asked Dorothy.

"Why, it is after midnight," said the King, "and that strikes me as being late enough. There is neither night nor day in my kingdom, because it is under the earth's surface, where the sun does not shine. But we have to sleep, just the same as the up-stairs people do, and for my part I'm going to bed in a few minutes."

Indeed, it was not long after this that the private made his last guess. Of course he guessed wrongly, and of course he at once became an ornament. So the King was greatly pleased, and clapped his hands to summon his Chief Steward.

"Show these guests to some of the sleeping apartments," he commanded, "and be quick about it, too, for I'm dreadfully sleepy myself."

"You've no business to sit up so late," replied the Steward, gruffly. "You'll be as cross as a griffin tomorrow morning."

SOON SHE HAD FALLEN FAST ASLEEP

His Majesty made no answer to this remark, and the Chief Steward led Dorothy through another doorway into a long hall, from which several plain but comfortable sleeping rooms opened. The little girl was given the first room, and the Scarecrow and Tiktok the next—although they never slept—and the Lion and the Tiger the third. The Sawhorse hobbled after the Steward into a fourth room, to stand stiffly in the center of it until morning. Each night was rather a bore to the Scarecrow, Tiktok and the Sawhorse; but they had learned from experience to pass the time patiently and quietly, since all their friends who were made of flesh had to sleep and did not like to be disturbed.

When the Chief Steward had left them alone the Scarecrow remarked, sadly:

"I am in great sorrow over the loss of my old comrade, the Tin Woodman. We have had many dangerous adventures together, and escaped them all, and now it grieves me to know he has become an ornament, and is lost to me forever."

"He was al-ways an or-na-ment to so-ci-e-ty," said Tiktok.

"True; but now the Nome King laughs at him, and calls him the funniest ornament in all the palace. It will hurt my poor friend's pride to be laughed at," continued the Scarecrow, sadly.

"We will make rath-er ab-surd or-na-ments, our-selves, to-mor-row," observed the machine, in his monotonous voice.

Just then Dorothy ran into their room, in a state of great anxiety, crying:

"Where's Billina? Have you seen Billina? Is she here?"

"No," answered the Scarecrow.

"Then what has become of her?" asked the girl.

"Why, I thought she was with you," said the Scarecrow. "Yet I do not remember seeing the yellow hen since she picked up the crumbs of cake."

"We must have left her in the room where the King's throne is," decided Dorothy, and at once she turned and ran down the hall to the door through which they had entered. But it was fast closed and locked on the other side, and the heavy slab of rock proved to be so thick that no sound could pass through it. So Dorothy was forced to return to her chamber.

The Cowardly Lion stuck his head into her room to try to console the girl for the loss of her feathered friend.

"The yellow hen is well able to take care of her-self," said he; "so don't worry about her, but try to get all the sleep you can. It has been a long and weary day, and you need rest."

"I'll prob'ly get lots of rest tomorrow, when I become an orn'ment," said Dorothy, sleepily. But she lay down upon her couch, nevertheless, and in spite of all her worries was soon in the land of dreams.

Dorothy Tries to be Brave

Meantime the Chief Steward had returned to the throne room, where he said to the King:

"You are a fool to waste so much time upon these people."

"What!" cried his Majesty, in so enraged a voice that it awoke Billina, who was asleep under his throne. "How dare you call me a fool?"

"Because I like to speak the truth," said the Steward. "Why didn't you enchant them all at once, instead of allowing them to go one by one into the palace and guess which ornaments are the Queen of Ev and her children?"

"Why, you stupid rascal, it is more fun this way," returned the King, "and it serves to keep me amused for a long time."

"But suppose some of them happen to guess aright," persisted the Steward; "then you would lose your old ornaments and these new ones, too."

"There is no chance of their guessing aright," replied the monarch, with a laugh. "How could they know that the Queen of Ev and her family are all ornaments of a royal purple color?"

"But there are no other purple ornaments in the palace," said the Steward.

"There are many other colors, however, and the purple ones are scattered throughout the rooms, and are of many different shapes and sizes. Take my word for it, Steward, they will never think of choosing the purple ornaments."

Billina, squatting under the throne, had listened carefully to all this talk, and now chuckled softly to herself as she heard the King disclose his secret.

"Still, you are acting foolishly by running the chance," continued the Steward, roughly; "and it is still more foolish of you to transform all those people from Oz into green ornaments."

"I did that because they came from the Emerald

"HOW DARE YOU CALL ME A FOOL?"

City," replied the King; "and I had no green ornaments in my collection until now. I think they will look quite pretty, mixed with the others. Don't you?"

The Steward gave an angry grunt.

"Have your own way, since you are the King," he growled. "But if you come to grief through your carelessness, remember that I told you so. If I wore the magic belt which enables you to work all your transformations, and gives you so much other power, I am sure I would make a much wiser and better King than you are."

"Oh, cease your tiresome chatter!" commanded the King, getting angry again. "Because you are my Chief Steward you have an idea you can scold me as much as you please. But the very next time you become impudent, I will send you to work in the furnaces, and get another Nome to fill your place. Now follow me to my chamber, for I am going to bed. And see that I am wakened early tomorrow morning. I want to enjoy the fun of transforming the rest of these people into ornaments."

"What color will you make the Kansas girl?" asked the Steward.

"Gray, I think," said his Majesty.

"And the Scarecrow and the machine man?"

Dorothy Tries to be Brave

"Oh, they shall be of solid gold, because they are so ugly in real life."

Then the voices died away, and Billina knew that the King and his Steward had left the room. She fixed up some of her tail feathers that were not straight, and then tucked her head under her wing again and went to sleep.

In the morning Dorothy and the Lion and Tiger were given their breakfast in their rooms, and afterward joined the King in his throne room. The Tiger complained bitterly that he was half starved, and begged to go into the palace and become an ornament, so that he would no longer suffer the pangs of hunger.

"Haven't you had your breakfast?" asked the Nome King.

"Oh, I had just a bite," replied the beast. "But what good is a bite, to a hungry tiger?"

"He ate seventeen bowls of porridge, a platter full of fried sausages, eleven loaves of bread and twenty-one mince pies," said the Steward.

"What more do you want?" demanded the King.

"A fat baby. I want a fat baby," said the Hungry Tiger. "A nice, plump, juicy, tender, fat baby. But, of course, if I had one, my conscience would not allow me to eat it. So I'll have to be an ornament and forget my hunger."

"Impossible!" exclaimed the King. "I'll have no clumsy beasts enter my palace, to overturn and break all my pretty nick-nacks. When the rest of your friends are transformed you can return to the upper world, and go about your business."

"As for that, we have no business, when our friends are gone," said the Lion. "So we do not care much what becomes of us."

Dorothy begged to be allowed to go first into the palace, but Tiktok firmly maintained that the slave should face danger before the mistress. The Scarecrow agreed with him in that, so the Nome King opened the door for the machine man, who tramped into the palace to meet his fate. Then his Majesty returned to his throne and puffed his pipe so contentedly that a small cloud of smoke formed above his head.

Bye and bye he said:

"I'm sorry there are so few of you left. Very soon, now, my fun will be over, and then for amusement I shall have nothing to do but admire my new ornaments."

"It seems to me," said Dorothy, "that you are not so honest as you pretend to be."

THE NOME KING PUFFED HIS PIPE

"How's that?" asked the King.

"Why, you made us think it would be easy to guess what ornaments the people of Ev were changed into."

"It *is* easy," declared the monarch, "if one is a good guesser. But it appears that the members of your party are all poor guessers."

"What is Tiktok doing now?" asked the girl, uneasily.

"Nothing," replied the King, with a frown. "He is standing perfectly still, in the middle of a room."

"Oh, I expect he's run down," said Dorothy. "I forgot to wind him up this morning. How many guesses has he made?"

"All that he is allowed except one," answered the King. "Suppose you go in and wind him up, and then you can stay there and make your own guesses."

"All right," said Dorothy.

"It is my turn next," declared the Scarecrow.

"Why, you don't want to go away and leave me all alone, do you?" asked the girl. "Besides, if I go now I can wind up Tiktok, so that he can make his last guess."

"Very well, then," said the Scarecrow, with a sigh.

Dorothy Tries to be Brave

"Run along, little Dorothy, and may good luck go with you!"

So Dorothy, trying to be brave in spite of her fears, passed through the doorway into the gorgeous rooms of the palace. The stillness of the place awed her, at first, and the child drew short breaths, and pressed her hand to her heart, and looked all around with wondering eyes.

Yes, it was a beautiful place; but enchantments lurked in every nook and corner, and she had not yet grown accustomed to the wizardries of these fairy countries, so different from the quiet and sensible common-places of her own native land.

Slowly she passed through several rooms until she came upon Tiktok, standing motionless. It really seemed, then, that she had found a friend in this mysterious palace, so she hastened to wind up the machine man's action and speech and thoughts.

"Thank you, Dor-oth-y," were his first words. "I have now one more guess to make."

"Oh, be very careful, Tiktok; won't you?" cried the girl.

"Yes. But the Nome King has us in his power, and he has set a trap for us. I fear we are all lost." he answered.

"I fear so, too," said Dorothy, sadly.

"If Smith & Tin-ker had giv-en me a guess-ing clock-work at-tach-ment," continued Tiktok, "I might have de-fied the Nome King. But my thoughts are plain and sim-ple, and are not of much use in this case."

"Do the best you can," said Dorothy, encourag-ingly, "and if you fail I will watch and see what shape you are changed into."

So Tiktok touched a yellow glass vase that had daisies painted on one side, and he spoke at the same time the word "Ev."

In a flash the machine man had disappeared, and although the girl looked quickly in every direction, she could not tell which of the many ornaments the room contained had a moment before been her faithful friend and servant.

So all she could do was to accept the hopeless task set her, and make her guesses and abide by the result.

"It can't hurt very much," she thought, "for I haven't heard any of them scream or cry out—not even the poor officers. Dear me! I wonder if Uncle Henry or Aunt Em will ever know I have become an orn'ment in the Nome King's palace, and must stand forever and ever in one place and look pretty—'cept when I'm moved to be dusted.

It isn't the way I thought I'd turn out, at all; but I s'pose it can't be helped."

She walked through all the rooms once more, and examined with care all the objects they contained; but there were so many, they bewildered her, and she decided, after all, as Ozma had done, that it could be only guess work at the best, and that the chances were much against her guessing aright.

Timidly she touched an alabaster bowl and said: "Ev."

"That's one failure, anyhow," she thought. "But how am I to know which thing is enchanted, and which is not?"

Next she touched the image of a purple kitten that stood on the corner of a mantel, and as she pronounced the word "Ev" the kitten disappeared, and a pretty, fair-haired boy stood beside her. At the same time a bell rang somewhere in the distance, and as Dorothy started back, partly in surprise and partly in joy, the little one exclaimed:

"Where am I? And who are you? And what has happened to me?"

"Well, I declare!" said Dorothy. "I've really done it."

"Done what?" asked the boy.

"Saved myself from being an ornament," replied the girl, with a laugh, "and saved you from being forever a purple kitten."

"A purple kitten?" he repeated. "There *is* no such thing."

"I know," she answered. "But there was, a minute ago. Don't you remember standing on a corner of the mantel?"

Dorothy Tries to be Brave

"Of course not. I am a Prince of Ev, and my name is Evring," the little one announced, proudly. "But my father, the King, sold my mother and all her children to the cruel ruler of the Nomes, and after that I remember nothing at all."

"A purple kitten can't be 'spected to remember, Evring," said Dorothy. "But now you are yourself again, and I'm going to try to save some of your brothers and sisters, and perhaps your mother, as well. So come with me."

She seized the child's hand and eagerly hurried here and there, trying to decide which object to choose next. The third guess was another failure, and so was the fourth and the fifth.

Little Evring could not imagine what she was doing, but he trotted along beside her very willingly, for he liked the new companion he had found.

Dorothy's further quest proved unsuccessful; but after her first disappointment was over, the little girl was filled with joy and thankfulness to think that after all she had been able to save one member of the royal family of Ev, and could restore the little Prince to his sorrowing country. Now she might return to the terrible Nome King in safety, carrying with her the prize she had won in the person of the fair-haired boy.

So she retraced her steps until she found the entrance to the palace, and as she approached, the
massive doors of rock opened of their own accord,
allowing both Dorothy and Evring to pass the portals
and enter the throne room.

Billina Frightens the Nome King

Now when Dorothy had entered the palace to make her guesses and the Scarecrow was left with the Nome King, the two sat in moody silence for several minutes. Then the monarch exclaimed, in a tone of satisfaction:

"Very good!"

"Who is very good?" asked the Scarecrow.

"The machine man. He won't need to be wound up any more, for he has now become a very neat ornament. Very neat, indeed."

"How about Dorothy?" the Scarecrow enquired.

"Oh, she will begin to guess, pretty soon," said the King, cheerfully. "And then she will join my collection, and it will be your turn."

The good Scarecrow was much distressed by the thought that his little friend was about to suffer the fate of Ozma and the rest of their party; but while he sat in gloomy reverie a shrill voice suddenly cried:

"Kut, kut, kut—ka-daw-kutt!   Kut, kut, kut—ka-daw-kutt!"

The Nome King nearly jumped off his seat, he was so startled.

"Good gracious!   What's that?" he yelled.

"Why, it's Billina," said the Scarecrow.

"What do you mean by making a noise like that?" shouted the King, angrily, as the yellow hen came from under the throne and strutted proudly about the room.

"I've got a right to cackle, I guess," replied Billina. "I've just laid my egg.'

"What!   Laid an egg!   In my throne room! How dare you do such a thing?" asked the King, in a voice of fury.

"I lay eggs wherever I happen to be," said the hen, ruffling her feathers and then shaking them into place.

Billina Frightens the Nome King

"But—thunder-ation! Don't you know that eggs are poison?" roared the King, while his rock-colored eyes stuck out in great terror.

"Poison! well, I declare," said Billina, indignantly. "I'll have you know all my eggs are warranted strictly fresh and up to date. Poison, indeed!"

"You don't understand," retorted the little monarch, nervously. "Eggs belong only to the outside world—to the world on the earth's surface, where you came from. Here, in my underground kingdom, they are rank poison, as I said, and we Nomes can't bear them around."

"Well, you'll have to bear this one around," declared Billina; "for I've laid it."

"Where?" asked the King.

"Under your throne," said the hen.

The King jumped three feet into the air, so anxious was he to get away from the throne.

"Take it away! Take it away at once!" he shouted.

"I can't," said Billina. "I havn't any hands."

"I'll take the egg," said the Scarecrow. "I'm making a collection of Billina's eggs. There's one in my pocket now, that she laid yesterday."

Hearing this, the monarch hastened to put a good distance between himself and the Scarecrow, who was about to reach under the throne for the egg when the hen suddenly cried:

"Stop!"

"What's wrong?" asked the Scarecrow.

"Don't take the egg unless the King will allow me to enter the palace and guess as the others have done," said Billina.

"Pshaw!" returned the King. "You re only a hen. How could you guess my enchantments?"

"I can try, I suppose," said Billina. "And, if I fail, you will have another ornament."

"A pretty ornament you'd make, wouldn't you?" growled the King. "But you shall have your way. It will properly punish you for daring to lay an egg in my presence. After the Scarecrow is enchanted you shall follow him into the palace. But how will you touch the objects?"

"With my claws," said the hen; "and I can speak the word 'Ev' as plainly as anyone. Also I must have the right to guess the enchantments of my friends, and to release them if I succeed."

"Very well," said the King. "You have my promise."

"Then," said Billina to the Scarecrow, "you may get the egg."

He knelt down and reached underneath the

"DON'T YOU KNOW THAT EGGS ARE POISON?"

throne and found the egg, which he placed in another pocket of his jacket, fearing that if both eggs were in one pocket they would knock together and get broken.

Just then a bell above the throne rang briskly, and the King gave another nervous jump.

"Well, well!" said he, with a rueful face; "the girl has actually done it."

"Done what?" asked the Scarecrow.

"She has made one guess that is right, and broken one of my neatest enchantments. By ricketty, it's too bad! I never thought she would do it."

"Do I understand that she will now return to us in safety?" enquired the Scarecrow, joyfully wrinkling his painted face into a broad smile.

"Of course," said the King, fretfully pacing up and down the room. "I always keep my promises, no matter how foolish they are. But I shall make an ornament of the yellow hen to replace the one I have just lost."

"Perhaps you will, and perhaps you won't," murmured Billina, calmly. "I may surprise you by guessing right."

"Guessing right?" snapped the King. "How should you guess right, where your betters have failed, you stupid fowl?"

Billina Frightens the Nome King

Billina did not care to answer this question, and a moment later the doors flew open and Dorothy entered, leading the little Prince Evring by the hand.

The Scarecrow welcomed the girl with a close embrace, and he would have embraced Evring, too,

in his delight. But the little Prince was shy, and shrank away from the painted Scarecrow because he did not yet know his many excellent qualities.

But there was little time for the friends to talk, because the Scarecrow must now enter the palace.

"BY RICKETTY, IT'S TOO BAD!"

Billina Frightens the Nome King

Dorothy's success had greatly encouraged him, and they both hoped he would manage to make at least one correct guess.

However, he proved as unfortunate as the others except Dorothy, and although he took a good deal of time to select his objects, not one did the poor Scarecrow guess aright.

So he became a solid gold card-receiver, and the beautiful but terrible palace awaited it's next visitor.

"It's all over," remarked the King, with a sigh of satisfaction; "and it has been a very amusing performance, except for the one good guess the Kansas girl made. I am richer by a great many pretty ornaments.

"It is my turn, now," said Billina, briskly.

"Oh, I'd forgotten you," said the King. "But you needn't go if you don't wish to. I will be generous, and let you off."

"No you won't," replied the hen. "I insist upon having my guesses, as you promised."

"Then go ahead, you absurd feathered fool!" grumbled the King, and he caused the opening that led to the palace to appear once more.

"Don't go, Billina," said Dorothy, earnestly. "It isn't easy to guess those orn'ments, and only luck saved me from being one myself. Stay with me.

and we'll go back to the Land of Ev together. I'm sure this little Prince will give us a home."

"Indeed I will," said Evring, with much dignity.

"Don't worry, my dear," cried Billina, with a cluck that was meant for a laugh. "I may not be human, but I'm no fool, if I *am* a chicken."

"Oh, Billina!" said Dorothy, "you haven't been a chicken in a long time. Not since you—you've been—grown up."

"Perhaps that's true," answered Billina, thoughtfully. "But if a Kansas farmer sold me to some one, what would he call me?—a hen or a chicken!"

"You are not a Kansas farmer, Billina," replied the girl, "and you said—"

"Never mind that, Dorothy. I'm going. I won't say good-bye, because I'm coming back. Keep up your courage, for I'll see you a little later."

Then Billina gave several loud "cluck-clucks" that seemed to make the fat little King *more* nervous than ever, and marched through the entrance into the enchanted palace.

"I hope I've seen the last of *that* bird," declared the monarch, seating himself again in his throne and mopping the perspiration from his forehead with his rock-colored handkerchief. "Hens are bothersome

Billina Frightens the Nome King

enough at their best, but when they can talk they're simply dreadful."

"Billina's my friend," said Dorothy quietly. "She may not always be 'zactly polite; but she *means* well, I'm sure.'

Purple, Green and Gold

The yellow hen, stepping high and with an air of vast importance, walked slowly over the rich velvet carpets of the splendid palace, examining everything she met with her sharp little eyes.

Billina had a right to feel important; for she alone shared the Nome King's secret and knew how to tell the objects that were transformations from those that had never been alive. She was very sure that her guesses would be correct, but before she began to make them she was curious to behold all the magnificence of this underground palace, which was perhaps one of

Purple, Green and Gold

the most splendid and beautiful places in any fairy-land.

As she went through the rooms she counted the purple ornaments; and although some were small and hidden in queer places, Billina spied them all, and found the entire ten scattered about the various rooms. The green ornaments she did not bother to count, for she thought she could find them all when the time came.

Finally, having made a survey of the entire palace and enjoyed its splendor, the yellow hen returned to one of the rooms where she had noticed a large purple footstool. She placed a claw upon this and said "Ev," and at once the footstool vanished and a lovely lady, tall and slender and most beautifully robed, stood before her.

The lady's eyes were round with astonishment for a moment, for she could not remember her transformation, nor imagine what had restored her to life.

"Good morning, ma'am," said Billina, in her sharp voice. "You're looking quite well, considering your age."

"Who speaks?" demanded the Queen of Ev, drawing herself up proudly.

"Why, my name's Bill, by rights," answered the

hen, who was now perched upon the back of a chair; "although Dorothy has put scollops on it and made it Billina. But the name doesn't matter. I've saved you from the Nome King, and you are a slave no longer."

"Then I thank you for the gracious favor," said the Queen, with a graceful courtesy. "But, my children—tell me, I beg of you—where are my children?" and she clasped her hands in anxious entreaty.

"Don't worry," advised Billina, pecking at a tiny bug that was crawling over the chair back. "Just at present they are out of mischief and perfectly safe, for they can't even wiggle."

"What mean you, O kindly stranger?" asked the Queen, striving to repress her anxiety.

"They're enchanted," said Billina, "just as you have been—all, that is, except the little fellow Dorothy picked out. And the chances are that they have been good boys and girls for some time, because they couldn't help it."

"Oh, my poor darlings!" cried the Queen, with a sob of anguish.

"Not at all," returned the hen. "Don't let their condition make you unhappy, ma'am, because I'll soon have them crowding 'round to bother and

Purple, Green and Gold

worry you as naturally as ever. Come with me, if you please, and I'll show you how pretty they look."

She flew down from her perch and walked into the next room, the Queen following. As she passed a low table a small green grasshopper caught her eye, and instantly Billina pounced upon it and snapped it up in her sharp bill. For grasshoppers are a favorite food with hens, and they usually must be caught quickly, before they can hop away. It might easily have been the end of Ozma of Oz, had she been a real grasshopper instead of an emerald one. But Billina found the grasshopper hard and lifeless, and suspecting it was not good to eat she quickly dropped it instead of letting it slide down her throat.

"I might have known better," she muttered to herself, "for where there is no grass there can be no live grasshoppers. This is probably one of the King's transformations."

A moment later she approached one of the purple ornaments, and while the Queen watched her curiously the hen broke the Nome King's enchantment and a sweet-faced girl, whose golden hair fell in a cloud over her shoulders, stood beside them.

"Evanna!" cried the Queen, "my own Evanna!"

and she clasped the girl to her bosom and covered her face with kisses.

"That's all right," said Billina, contentedly. "Am I a good guesser, Mr. Nome King? Well, I guess!"

Then she disenchanted another girl, whom the Queen addressed as Evrose, and afterwards a boy named Evardo, who was older than his brother Evring. Indeed, the yellow hen kept the good Queen exclaiming and embracing for some time, until five Princesses and four Princes, all looking very much alike except for the difference in size, stood in a row beside their happy mother.

The Princesses were named, Evanna, Evrose, Evella, Evirene and Evedna, while the Princes were Evrob, Evington, Evardo and Evroland. Of these Evardo was the eldest and would inherit his father's throne and be crowned King of Ev when he returned to his own country. He was a grave and quiet youth, and would doubtless rule his people wisely and with justice.

Billina, having restored all of the royal family of Ev to their proper forms, now began to select the green ornaments which were the transformations of the people of Oz. She had little trouble in finding these, and before long all the twenty-six officers, as well as the private, were gathered around the

THE QUEEN OF EV THANKS **BILLINA**

yellow hen, joyfully congratulating her upon their release. The thirty-seven people who were now alive in the rooms of the palace knew very well that they owed their freedom to the cleverness of the yellow hen, and they were earnest in thanking her for saving them from the magic of the Nome King.

"Now," said Billina, "I must find Ozma. She is sure to be here, somewhere, and of course she is green, being from Oz. So look around, you stupid soldiers and help me in my search."

For a while, however, they could discover nothing more that was green. But the Queen, who had kissed all her nine children once more and could now find time to take an interest in what was going on, said to the hen:

"Mayhap, my gentle friend, it is the grasshopper whom you seek."

"Of course it's the grasshopper!" exclaimed Billina. "I declare, I'm nearly as stupid as these brave soldiers. Wait here for me, and I'll go back and get it."

So she went into the room where she had seen the grasshopper, and presently Ozma of Oz, as lovely and dainty as ever, entered and approached the Queen of Ev, greeting her as one high born princess greets another.

Purple, Green and Gold

"But where are my friends, the Scarecrow and the Tin Woodman?" asked the girl Ruler, when these courtesies had been exchanged.

"I'll hunt them up," replied Billina. "The Scarecrow is solid gold, and so is Tiktok; but I don't exactly know what the Tin Woodman is, because the Nome King said he had been transformed into something funny."

Ozma eagerly assisted the hen in her quest, and soon the Scarecrow and the machine man, being ornaments of shining gold, were discovered and restored to their accustomed forms. But, search as they might, in no place could they find a funny ornament that might be the transformation of the Tin Woodman.

"Only one thing can be done," said Ozma, at last, "and that is to return to the Nome King and oblige him to tell us what has become of our friend."

"Perhaps he won't," suggested Billina.

"He must," returned Ozma, firmly. "The King has not treated us honestly, for under the mask of fairness and good nature he entrapped us all, and we would have been forever enchanted had not our wise and clever friend, the yellow hen, found a way to save us."

"The King is a villain," declared the Scarecrow.

"His laugh is worse than another man's frown," said the private, with a shudder.

"I thought he was hon-est, but I was mis-tak-en," remarked Tiktok. "My thoughts are us-u-al-ly cor-rect, but it is Smith & Tin-ker's fault if they some-times go wrong or do not work prop-er-ly."

"Smith & Tinker made a very good job of you," said Ozma, kindly. "I do not think they should be blamed if you are not quite perfect."

"Thank you," replied Tiktok.

"Then," said Billina, in her brisk little voice, "let us all go back to the Nome King, and see what he has to say for himself."

So they started for the entrance, Ozma going first, with the Queen and her train of little Princes and Princesses following. Then came Tiktok, and the Scarecrow with Billina perched upon his straw-stuffed shoulder. The twenty-seven officers and the private brought up the rear.

As they reached the hall the doors flew open before them; but then they all stopped and stared into the domed cavern with faces of astonishment and dismay. For the room was filled with the mail-clad warriors of the Nome King, rank after rank standing in orderly array. The electric lights upon their brows gleamed brightly, their battle-axes

Purple, Green and Gold

were poised as if to strike down their foes; yet they remained motionless as statues, awaiting the word of command.

And in the center of this terrible army sat the little King upon his throne of rock. But he neither smiled nor laughed. Instead, his face was distorted with rage, and most dreadful to behold.

The Scarecrow Wins the Fight

After Billina had entered the palace Dorothy and Ev-ring sat down to await the success or failure of her mission, and the Nome King occupied his throne and smoked his long pipe for a while in a cheerful and contented mood.

Then the bell above the throne, which sounded whenever an enchantment was broken, began to ring, and the King gave a start of annoyance and exclaimed, "Rocketty-ricketts!"

When the bell rang a second time the King shouted angrily, "Smudge and blazes!" and at a third ring he screamed in a fury, "Hippikaloric!"

which must be a dreadful word because we don't know what it means.

After that the bell went on ringing time after time; but the King was now so violently enraged that he could not utter a word, but hopped out of his throne and all around the room in a mad frenzy, so that he reminded Dorothy of a jumping-jack.

The girl was, for her part, filled with joy at every peal of the bell, for it announced the fact that Billina had transformed one more ornament into a living person. Dorothy was also amazed at Billina's success, for she could not imagine how the yellow hen was able to guess correctly from all the bewildering number of articles clustered in the rooms of the palace. But after she had counted ten, and the bell continued to ring, she knew that not only the royal family of Ev, but Ozma and her followers also, were being restored to their natural forms, and she was so delighted that the antics of the angry King only made her laugh merrily.

Perhaps the little monarch could not be more furious than he was before, but the girl's laughter nearly drove him frantic, and he roared at her like a savage beast. Then, as he found that all his enchantments were likely to be dispelled and his victims every one set free, he suddenly ran to the little door that opened upon the balcony and gave the shrill whistle that summoned his warriors.

At once the army filed out of the gold and silver doors in great numbers, and marched up a winding stairs and into the throne room, led by a stern featured Nome who was their captain. When they had nearly filled the throne room they formed ranks in the big underground cavern below, and then stood still until they were told what to do next.

Dorothy had pressed back to one side of the cavern when the warriors entered, and now she stood holding little Prince Evring's hand while the great Lion crouched upon one side and the enormous Tiger crouched an the other side.

"Seize that girl!" shouted the King to his captain, and a group of warriors sprang forward to obey. But both the Lion and Tiger snarled so fiercely and bared their strong, sharp teeth so threateningly, that the men drew back in alarm.

"Don't mind them!" cried the Nome King; "they cannot leap beyond the places where they now stand."

"But they can bite those who attempt to touch the girl," said the captain.

"I'll fix that," answered the King. "I'll enchant them again, so that they can't open their jaws."

The Scarecrow Wins the Fight

He stepped out of the throne to do this, but just then the Sawhorse ran up behind him and gave the fat monarch a powerful kick with both his wooden hind legs.

"Ow! Murder! Treason!" yelled the King, who had been hurled against several of his warriors and was considerably bruised. "Who did that?"

"I did," growled the Sawhorse, viciously. "You let Dorothy alone, or I'll kick you again."

"We'll see about that," replied the King, and at once he waved his hand toward the Sawhorse and muttered a magical word. "Aha!" he continued; "*now* let us see you move, you wooden mule!"

But in spite of the magic the Sawhorse moved; and he moved so quickly toward the King, that the fat little man could not get out of his way. Thump— *bang!* came the wooden heels, right against his round body, and the King flew into the air and fell upon the head of his captain, who let him drop flat upon the ground.

"Well, well!" said the King, sitting up and looking surprised. "Why didn't my magic belt work, I wonder?"

"The creature is made of wood," replied the captain. "Your magic will not work on wood, you know."

"Ah, I'd forgotten that," said the King, getting up and limping to his throne. "Very well, let the girl alone. She can't escape us, anyway."

The warriors, who had been rather confused by these incidents, now formed their ranks again, and the Sawhorse pranced across the room to Dorothy and took a position beside the Hungry Tiger.

At that moment the doors that led to the palace flew open and the people of Ev and the people of Oz were disclosed to view. They paused, astonished, at sight of the warriors and the angry Nome King, seated in their midst.

"Surrender!" cried the King, in a loud voice. "You are my prisoners."

"Go 'long!" answered Billina, from the Scarecrow's shoulder. "You promised me that if I guessed correctly my friends and I might depart in safety. And you always keep your promises."

"I said you might leave the palace in safety," retorted the King; "and so you may, but you cannot leave my dominions. You are my prisoners, and I will hurl you all into my underground dungeons, where the volcanic fires glow and the molten lava flows in every direction, and the air is hotter than blue blazes."

"That will be the end of me, all right," said the

"HELP, HELP!" SCREAMED THE KING

Scarecrow, sorrowfully. "One small blaze, blue or green, is enough to reduce me to an ash-heap."

"Do you surrender?" demanded the King.

Billina whispered something in the Scarecrow's ear that made him smile and put his hands in his jacket pockets.

"No!" returned Ozma, boldly answering the King. Then she said to her army:

"Forward, my brave soldiers, and fight for your Ruler and yourselves, unto death!"

"Pardon me, Most Royal Ozma," replied one of her generals; "but I find that I and my brother officers all suffer from heart disease, and the slightest excitement might kill us. If we fight we may get excited. Would it not be well for us to avoid this grave danger?"

"Soldiers should not have heart disease," said Ozma.

"Private soldiers are not, I believe, afflicted that way," declared another general, twirling his moustache thoughtfully. "If your Royal Highness desires, we will order our private to attack yonder warriors."

"Do so," replied Ozma.

"For-ward—march!" cried all the generals, with one voice. "For-ward—march!" yelled the colonels. "For-ward—march!" shouted the majors.

The Scarecrow Wins the Fight

"For-ward—march!" commanded the captains.

And at that the private leveled his spear and dashed furiously upon the foe.

The captain of the Nomes was so surprised by this sudden onslaught that he forgot to command his warriors to fight, so that the ten men in the first row, who stood in front of the private's spear, fell over like so many toy soldiers. The spear could not go through their steel armor, however, so the warriors scrambled to their feet again, and by that time the private had knocked over another row of them.

Then the captain brought down his battle-axe with such a strong blow that the private's spear was shattered and knocked from his grasp, and he was helpless to fight any longer.

The Nome King had left his throne and pressed through his warriors to the front ranks, so he could see what was going on; but as he faced Ozma and her friends the Scarecrow, as if aroused to action by the valor of the private, drew one of Billina's eggs from his right jacket pocket and hurled it straight at the little monarch's head.

It struck him squarely in his left eye, where the egg smashed and scattered, as eggs will, and covered his face and hair and beard with its sticky contents.

"Help, help!" screamed the King, clawing with his fingers at the egg, in a struggle to remove it.

"An egg! an egg! Run for your lives!" shouted the captain of the Nomes, in a voice of horror.

And how they *did* run! The warriors fairly tumbled over one another in their efforts to escape the fatal poison of that awful egg, and those who could not rush down the winding stair fell off the balcony into the great cavern beneath, knocking over those who stood below them.

Even while the King was still yelling for help his throne room became emptied of every one of his warriors, and before the monarch had managed to clear the egg away from his left eye the Scarecrow threw the second egg against his right eye, where it smashed and blinded him entirely. The King was unable to flee because he could not see which way to run; so he stood still and howled and shouted and screamed in abject fear.

While this was going on, Billina flew over to Dorothy, and perching herself upon the Lion's back the hen whispered eagerly to the girl:

"Get his belt! Get the Nome King's jeweled belt! It unbuckles in the back. Quick, Dorothy— quick!"

The Fate of the Tin Woodman

Dorothy obeyed. She ran at once behind the Nome King, who was still trying to free his eyes from the egg, and in a twinkling she had unbuckled his splendid jeweled belt and carried it away with her to her place beside the Tiger and Lion, where, because she did not know what else to do with it, she fastened it around her own slim waist.

Just then the Chief Steward rushed in with a sponge and a bowl of water, and began mopping away the broken eggs from his master's face. In a few minutes, and while all the party stood looking on, the King regained the use of his eyes, and the first thing he did was to glare wickedly upon the Scarecrow and exclaim:

"I'll make you suffer for this, you hay-stuffed dummy! Don't you know eggs are poison to Nomes?"

"Really," said the Scarecrow, "they *don't* seem to agree with you, although I wonder why."

"They were strictly fresh and above suspicion," said Billina. "You ought to be glad to get them."

"I'll transform you all into scorpions!" cried the King, angrily, and began waving his arms and muttering magic words.

But none of the people became scorpions, so the King stopped and looked at them in surprise.

"What's wrong?" he asked.

"Why, you are not wearing your magic belt," replied the Chief Steward, after looking the King over carefully. "Where is it?" What have you done with it?"

The Nome King clapped his hand to his waist, and his rock colored face turned white as chalk.

"It's gone," he cried, helplessly. "It's gone, and I am ruined!"

Dorothy now stepped forward and said:

"Royal Ozma, and you, Queen of Ev, I welcome you and your people back to the land of the living.

The Fate of the Tin Woodman

Billina has saved you from your troubles, and now we will leave this drea'ful place, and return to Ev as soon as poss'ble."

While the child spoke they could all see that she wore the magic belt, and a great cheer went up from all her friends, which was led by the voices of the Scarecrow and the private. But the Nome King did not join them. He crept back onto his throne like a whipped dog, and lay there bitterly bemoaning his defeat.

"But we have not yet found my faithful follower, the Tin Woodman, "said Ozma to Dorothy, "and without him I do not wish to go away."

"Nor I," replied Dorothy, quickly. "Wasn't he in the palace?"

"He must be there," said Billina; "but I had no clew to guide me in guessing the Tin Woodman, so I must have missed him."

"We will go back into the rooms," said Dorothy. "This magic belt, I am sure, will help us to find our dear old friend."

So she re-entered the palace, the doors of which still stood open, and everyone followed her except the Nome King, the Queen of Ev and Prince Evring. The mother had taken the little Prince in her lap and was fondling and kissing him lovingly, for he was her youngest born.

But the others went with Dorothy, and when she came to the middle of the first room the girl waved her hand, as she had seen the King do, and commanded the Tin Woodman, whatever form he might then have, to resume his proper shape. No result followed this attempt, so Dorothy went into another room and repeated it, and so through all the rooms of the palace. Yet the Tin Woodman did not appear to them, nor could they imagine which among the thousands of ornaments was their transformed friend.

Sadly they returned to the throne room, where the King, seeing that they had met with failure, jeered at Dorothy, saying:

"You do not know how to use my belt, so it is of no use to you. Give it back to me and I will let you go free—you and all the people who came with you. As for the royal family of Ev, they are my slaves, and shall remain here."

"I shall keep the belt," said Dorothy.

"But how can you escape, without my consent?" asked the King.

"Easily enough," answered the girl. "All we need to do is to walk out the way that we came in."

DOROTHY AND BILLINA ARGUE WITH THE KING

"Oh, that's all, is it?" sneered the King. "Well, where is the passage through which you entered this room?"

They all looked around, but could not discover the place, for it had long since been closed. Dorothy, however, would not be dismayed. She waved her hand toward the seemingly solid wall of the cavern and said:

"I command the passage to open!"

Instantly the order was obeyed; the opening appeared and the passage lay plainly before them.

The King was amazed, and all the others overjoyed.

"Why, then, if the belt obeys you, were we unable to discover the Tin Woodman?" asked Ozma.

"I can't imagine," said Dorothy.

"See here, girl," proposed the King, eagerly; "give me the belt, and I will tell you what shape the Tin Woodman was changed into, and then you can easily find him."

Dorothy hesitated, but Billina cried out:

"Don't you do it! If the Nome King gets the belt again he will make every one of us prisoners, for we will be in his power. Only by keeping the belt, Dorothy, will you ever be able to leave this place in safety."

The Fate of the Tin Woodman

"I think that is true," said the Scarecrow. "But I have another idea, due to my excellent brains. Let Dorothy transform the King into a goose-egg unless he agrees to go into the palace and bring out to us the ornament which is our friend Nick Chopper, the Tin Woodman."

"A goose-egg!" echoed the horrified King. "How dreadful!"

"Well, a goose-egg you will be unless you go and fetch us the ornament we want," declared Billina, with a joyful chuckle.

"You can see for yourself that Dorothy, is able to use the magic belt all right," added the Scarecrow.

The Nome King thought it over and finally consented, for he did not want to be a goose-egg. So he went into the palace to get the ornament which was the transformation of the Tin Woodman, and they all awaited his return with considerable impatience, for they were anxious to leave this underground cavern and see the sunshine once more. But when the Nome King came back he brought nothing with him except a puzzled and anxious expression upon his face.

"He's gone!" he said. "The Tin Woodman is nowhere in the palace."

"Are you sure?" asked Ozma, sternly.

"I'm very sure," answered the King, trembling, "for I know just what I transformed him into, and exactly where he stood. But he is not there, and please don't change me into a goose-egg, because I've done the best I could."

They were all silent for a time, and then Dorothy said:

"There is no use punishing the Nome King any

The Fate of the Tin Woodman

more, and I'm 'fraid we'll have to go away without our friend."

"If he is not here, we cannot rescue him," agreed the Scarecrow, sadly. "Poor Nick! I wonder what has become of him."

"And he owed me six weeks back pay!" said one of the generals, wiping the tears from his eyes with his gold-laced coat sleeve.

Very sorrowfully they determined to return to the upper world without their former companion, and so Ozma gave the order to begin the march through the passage.

The army went first, and then the royal family of Ev, and afterward came Dorothy, Ozma, Billina, the Scarecrow and Tiktok.

They left the Nome King scowling at them from his throne, and had no thought of danger until Ozma chanced to look back and saw a large number of the warriors following them in full chase, with their swords and spears and axes raised to strike down the fugitives as soon as they drew near enough.

Evidently the Nome King had made this last attempt to prevent their escaping him; but it did him no good, for when Dorothy saw the danger they were in she stopped and waved her hand and whispered a command to the magic belt.

Instantly the foremost warriors became eggs, which rolled upon the floor of the cavern in such numbers that those behind could not advance without stepping upon them. But, when they saw the eggs, all desire to advance departed from the warriors, and they turned and fled madly into the cavern, and refused to go back again.

Our friends had no farther trouble in reaching the end of the passage, and soon were standing in the outer air upon the gloomy path between the

The Fate of the Tin Woodman

two high mountains. But the way to Ev lay plainly before them, and they fervently hoped that they had seen the last of the Nome King and of his dreadful palace.

The cavalcade was led by Ozma, mounted on the Cowardly Lion, and the Queen of Ev, who rode upon the back of the Tiger. The children of the Queen walked behind her, hand in hand. Dorothy rode the Sawhorse, while the Scarecrow walked and commanded the army in the absence of the Tin Woodman.

Presently the way began to lighten and more of the sunshine to come in between the two mountains. And before long they heard the "thump! thump! thump!" of the giant's hammer upon the road.

"How may we pass the monstrous man of iron?" asked the Queen, anxious for the safety of her children. But Dorothy solved the problem by a word to the magic belt.

The giant paused, with his hammer held motionless in the air, thus allowing the entire party to pass between his cast-iron legs in safety.

The King of Ev

If there were any shifting, rock-colored Nomes on the mountain side now, they were silent and respect-ful, for our adventurers were not annoyed, as before, by their impudent laughter. Really the Nomes had nothing to laugh at, since the defeat of their King.

On the other side they found Ozma's golden chariot, standing as they had left it. Soon the Lion and the Tiger were harnessed to the beautiful chariot, in which was enough room for Ozma and the Queen and six of the royal children.

Little Evring preferred to ride with Dorothy upon the Sawhorse, which had a long back. The Prince had recovered from his shyness and had become very fond of the girl who had rescued him, so they were fast friends and chatted pleasantly together as they rode along. Billina was also perched upon the head of the wooden steed, which seemed not to mind the added weight in the least, and the boy was full of wonder that a hen could talk, and say such sensible things.

When they came to the gulf, Ozma's magic carpet carried them all over in safety; and now they began to pass the trees, in which birds were singing; and the breeze that was wafted to them from the farms of Ev was spicy with flowers and new-mown hay; and the sunshine fell full upon them, to warm them and drive away from their bodies the chill and dampness of the underground kingdom of the Nomes.

"I would be quite content," said the Scarecrow to Tiktok, "were only the Tin Woodman with us. But it breaks my heart to leave him behind."

"He was a fine fel-low," replied Tiktok, "although his ma-ter-i-al was not ve-ry du-ra-ble."

"Oh, tin is an excellent material," the Scarecrow hastened to say; "and if anything ever happened to poor Nick Chopper he was always easily soldered.

Besides, he did not have to be wound up, and was not liable to get out of order."

"I some-times wish," said Tiktok, "that I was stuffed with straw, as you are. It is hard to be made of cop-per."

"I have no reason to complain of my lot," replied the Scarecrow. "A little fresh straw, now and then, makes me as good as new. But I can never be the polished gentleman that my poor departed friend, the Tin Woodman, was.'

You may be sure the royal children of Ev and their Queen mother were delighted at seeing again their beloved country; and when the towers of the palace of Ev came into view they could not forbear cheering at the sight. Little Evring, riding in front of Dorothy, was so overjoyed that he took a curious tin whistle from his pocket and blew a shrill blast that made the Sawhorse leap and prance in sudden alarm.

"What is that?" asked Billina, who had been obliged to flutter her wings in order to keep her seat upon the head of the frightened Sawhorse.

"That's my whistle," said Prince Evring, holding it out upon his hand.

It was in the shape of a little fat pig, made of tin and painted green. The whistle was in the tail of the pig.

"Where did you get it?" asked the yellow hen, closely examining the toy with her bright eyes.

"Why, I picked it up in the Nome King's palace, while Dorothy was making her guesses, and I put it in my pocket," answered the little Prince.

Billina laughed; or at least she made the peculiar cackle that served her for a laugh.

"No wonder I couldn't find the Tin Woodman," she said; and no wonder the magic belt didn't make him appear, or the King couldn't find him, either!"

"What do you mean?" questioned Dorothy.

"Why, the Prince had him in his pocket," cried Billina, cackling again.

"I did not!" protested little Evring. "I only took the whistle."

"Well, then, watch me," returned the hen, and reaching out a claw she touched the whistle and said "Ev."

Swish!

"Good afternoon," said the Tin Woodman, taking off his funnel cap and bowing to Dorothy and the Prince. "I think I must have been asleep for the first time since I was made of tin, for I do not remember our leaving the Nome King."

"You have been enchanted," answered the girl, throwing an arm around her old friend and hugging him tight in her joy. "But it's all right, now."

"I want my whistle!" said the little Prince, beginning to cry.

"Hush!" cautioned Billina. "The whistle is lost, but you may have another when you get home."

The Scarecrow had fairly thrown himself upon the bosom of his old comrade, so surprised and delighted was he to see him again, and Tiktok squeezed the Tin Woodman's hand so earnestly that he dented some of his fingers. Then they had to make way

"YOUR FUTURE RULER, KING EVARDO FIFTEENTH"

for Ozma to welcome the tin man, and the army caught sight of him and set up a cheer, and everybody was delighted and happy.

For the Tin Woodman was a great favorite with all who knew him, and his sudden recovery after they had thought he was lost to them forever was indeed a pleasant surprise.

Before long the cavalcade arrived at the royal palace, where a great crowd of people had gathered to welcome their Queen and her ten children. There was much shouting and cheering, and the people threw flowers in their path, and every face wore a happy smile.

They found the Princess Langwidere in her mirrored chamber, where she was admiring one of her handsomest heads—one with rich chestnut hair, dreamy walnut eyes and a shapely hickorynut nose. She was very glad to be relieved of her duties to the people of Ev, and the Queen graciously permitted her to retain her rooms and her cabinet of heads as long as she lived.

Then the Queen took her eldest son out upon a balcony that overlooked the crowd of subjects gathered below, and said to them:

"Here is your future ruler, King Evardo Fifteenth. He is fifteen years of age, has fifteen silver buckles on his jacket and is the fifteenth Evardo to rule the land of Ev."

The people shouted their approval fifteen times, and even the Wheelers, some of whom were present, loudly promised to obey the new King.

So the Queen placed a big crown of gold, set with rubies, upon Evardo's head, and threw an ermine robe over his shoulders, and proclaimed him King; and he bowed gratefully to all his subjects and then went away to see if he could find any cake in the royal pantry.

Ozma of Oz and her people, as well as Dorothy, Tiktok and Billina, were splendidly entertained by the Queen mother, who owed all her happiness to their kind offices; and that evening the yellow hen was publicly presented with a beautiful necklace of pearls and sapphires, as a token of esteem from the new King.

The Emerald City

Dorothy

decided to accept Oz-
ma's invitation to return
with her to the Land of Oz.
There was no greater chance
of her getting home from Ev
than from Oz, and the little girl
was anxious to see once more the
country where she had encountered
such wonderful adventures. By this
time Uncle Henry would have reached
Australia in his ship, and had probably
given her up for lost; so he couldn't worry
any more than he did if she stayed away from
him a while longer. So she would go to Oz.

They bade good-bye to the people of Ev, and
the King promised Ozma that he would ever be

grateful to her and render the Land of Oz any service that might lie within his power.

And then they approached the edge of the dangerous desert, and Ozma threw down the magic carpet, which at once unrolled far enough for all of them to walk upon it without being crowded.

Tiktok, claiming to be Dorothy's faithful follower because he belonged to her, had been permitted to join the party, and before they started the girl wound up his machinery as far as possible, and the copper man stepped off as briskly as any one of them.

Ozma also invited Billina to visit the Land of Oz, and the yellow hen was glad enough to go where new sights and scenes awaited her.

They began the trip across the desert early in the morning, and as they stopped only long enough for Billina to lay her daily egg, before sunset they espied the green slopes and wooded hills of the beautiful Land of Oz. They entered it in the Munchkin territory, and the King of the Munchkins met them at the border and welcomed Ozma with great respect, being very pleased by her safe return. For Ozma of Oz ruled the King of the Munchkins, the King of the Winkies, the King of the Quadlings and the King of the Gillikins just as those kings ruled their own people; and this supreme ruler of the Land of Oz lived in a great town of her own, called the Emerald City, which was in the exact center of the four kingdoms of the Land of Oz.

The Munchkin king entertained them at his palace that night, and in the morning they set out for the Emerald City, travelling over a road of yellow brick that led straight to the jewel-studded gates. Everywhere the people turned out to greet their beloved Ozma, and to hail joyfully the Scarecrow, the Tin Woodman and the Cowardly Lion, who were popular favorites.   Dorothy, too, remembered some of the people, who had befriended her on the occasion of her first visit to Oz, and they were well pleased to see the little Kansas girl again, and showered her with compliments and good wishes.

At one place, where they stopped to refresh themselves, Ozma accepted a bowl of milk from the hands of a pretty dairy-maid.   Then she looked at the girl more closely, and exclaimed:

"Why, it's Jinjur—isn't it!"

"Yes, your Highness," was the reply, as Jinjur dropped a low curtsy. And Dorothy looked wonderingly at this lively appearing person, who had once assembled an army of women and driven the Scarecrow from the throne of the Emerald City, and even fought a battle with the powerful army of Glinda the Sorceress.

"I've married a man who owns nine cows," said Jinjur to Ozma, "and now I am happy and con-

tented and willing to lead a quiet life and mind my own business."

"Where is your husband?" asked Ozma.

"He is in the house, nursing a black eye," replied Jinjur, calmly. "The foolish man would insist upon milking the red cow when I wanted him to milk the white one; but he will know better next time, I am sure."

Then the party moved on again, and after crossing a broad river on a ferry and passing many fine farm houses that were dome shaped and painted a pretty green color, they came in sight of a large building that was covered with flags and bunting.

"I don't remember that building," said Dorothy. "What is it?"

"That is the College of Art and Athletic Perfection," replied Ozma. "I had it built quite recently, and the Woggle-Bug is it's president. It keeps him busy, and the young men who attend the college are no worse off than they were before. You see, in this country are a number of youths who do not like to work, and the college is an excellent place for them."

And now they came in sight of the Emerald City, and the people flocked out to greet their lovely ruler. There were several bands and many officers and officials of the realm, and a crowd of citizens in their holiday attire.

Thus the beautiful Ozma was escorted by a brilliant procession to her royal city, and so great was the cheering that she was obliged to constantly bow to the right and left to acknowledge the greetings of her subjects.

That evening there was a grand reception in the

"I PROMOTE YOU TO BE CAPTAIN-GENERAL

royal palace, attended by the most important persons of Oz, and Jack Pumpkinhead, who was a little over-ripe but still active, read an address congratulating Ozma of Oz upon the success of her generous mission to rescue the royal family of a neighboring kingdom.

Then magnificent gold medals set with precious stones were presented to each of the twenty-six officers; and the Tin Woodman was given a new axe studded with diamonds; and the Scarecrow received a silver jar of complexion powder. Dorothy was presented with a pretty coronet and made a Princess of Oz, and Tiktok received two bracelets set with eight rows of very clear and sparkling emeralds.

Afterward they sat down to a splendid feast, and Ozma put Dorothy at her right and Billina at her left, where the hen sat upon a golden roost and ate from a jeweled platter. Then were placed the Scarecrow, the Tin Woodman and Tiktok, with baskets of lovely flowers before them, because they did not require food. The twenty-six officers were at the lower end of the table, and the Lion and the Tiger also had seats, and were served on golden platters, that held a half a bushel at one time.

The wealthiest and most important citizens of

the Emerald City were proud to wait upon these famous adventurers, and they were assisted by a sprightly little maid named Jellia Jamb, whom the Scarecrow pinched upon her rosy cheeks and seemed to know very well.

During the feast Ozma grew thoughtful, and suddenly she asked:

"Where is the private?"

"Oh, he is sweeping out the barracks," replied one of the generals, who was busy eating a leg of a turkey. "But I have ordered him a dish of bread and molasses to eat when his work is done."

"Let him be sent for," said the girl ruler.

While they waited for this command to be obeyed, she enquired:

"Have we any other privates in the armies?"

"Oh, yes," replied the Tin Woodman, "I believe there are three, altogether."

The private now entered, saluting his officers and the royal Ozma very respectfully.

"What is your name, my man?" asked the girl.

"Omby Amby," answered the private.

"Then, Omby Amby," said she, "I promote you to be Captain General of all the armies of my kingdom, and especially to be Commander of my Body Guard at the royal palace."

"It is very expensive to hold so many offices," said the private, hesitating. "I have no money with which to buy uniforms."

"You shall be supplied from the royal treasury," said Ozma.

Then the private was given a seat at the table, where the other officers welcomed him cordially, and the feasting and merriment were resumed.

Suddenly Jellia Jamb exclaimed:

"There is nothing more to eat! The Hungry Tiger has consumed everything!"

"But that is not the worst of it," declared the Tiger, mournfully. "Somewhere or somehow, I've actually lost my appetite!"

Dorothy's Magic Belt

Dorothy passed several very happy weeks in the Land of Oz as the guest of the royal Ozma, who delighted to please and interest the little Kansas girl. Many new acquaintances were formed and many old ones renewed, and wherever she went Dorothy found herself among friends.

One day, however, as she sat in Ozma's private room, she noticed hanging upon the wall a picture which constantly changed in appearance, at one time showing a meadow and at another time a forest, a lake or a village.

"How curious!" she exclaimed, after watching the shifting scenes for a few moments.

"Yes," said Ozma, "that is really a wonderful invention in magic. If I wish to see any part of the world or any person living, I need only express the wish and it is shown in the picture."

"May I use it?" asked Dorothy, eagerly.

"Of course, my dear."

"Then I'd like to see the old Kansas farm, and Aunt Em," said the girl.

Instantly the well remembered farmhouse appeared in the picture, and Aunt Em could be seen quite plainly. She was engaged in washing dishes by the kitchen window and seemed quite well and contented. The hired men and the teams were in the harvest fields behind the house, and the corn and wheat seemed to the child to be in prime condition. On the side porch Dorothy's pet dog, Toto, was lying fast asleep in the sun, and to her surprise old Speckles was running around with a brood of twelve new chickens trailing after her.

"Everything seems all right at home," said Dorothy, with a sigh of relief. "Now I wonder what Uncle Henry is doing."

The scene in the picture at once shifted to Australia, where, in a pleasant room in Sydney,

Dorothy's Magic Belt

Uncle Henry was seated in an easy chair, solemnly smoking his briar pipe. He looked sad and lonely, and his hair was now quite white and his hands and face thin and wasted.

"Oh!" cried Dorothy, in an anxious voice, "I'm sure Uncle Henry isn't getting any better, and it's because he is worried about me. Ozma, dear, I must go to him at once!"

"How can you?" asked Ozma.

"I don't know," replied Dorothy; "but let us go to Glinda the Good. I'm sure she will help me, and advise me how to get to Uncle Henry."

Ozma readily agreed to this plan and caused the Sawhorse to be harnessed to a pretty green and pink phaeton, and the two girls rode away to visit the famous sorceress.

Glinda received them graciously, and listened to Dorothy's story with attention.

"I have the magic belt, you know," said the little girl. "If I buckled it around my waist and commanded it to take me to Uncle Henry, wouldn't it do it?"

"I think so," replied Glinda, with a smile.

"And then," continued Dorothy, "if I ever wanted to come back here again, the belt would bring me."

"THAT IS A WISE PLAN," REPLIED GLINDA

Dorothy's Magic Belt

"In that you are wrong," said the sorceress. "The belt has magical powers only while it is in some fairy country, such as the Land of Oz, or the Land of Ev. Indeed, my little friend, were you to wear it and wish yourself in Australia, with your uncle, the wish would doubtless be fulfilled, because it was made in fairyland. But you would not find the magic belt around you when you arrived at your destination."

"What would become of it?" asked the girl.

"It would be lost, as were your silver shoes when you visited Oz before, and no one would ever see it again. It seems too bad to destroy the use of the magic belt in that way, doesn't it?"

"Then," said Dorothy, after a moment's thought, "I will give the magic belt to Ozma, for she can use it in her own country. And she can wish me transported to Uncle Henry without losing the belt."

"That is a wise plan," replied Glinda.

So they rode back to the Emerald City, and on the way it was arranged that every Saturday morning Ozma would look at Dorothy in her magic picture, wherever the little girl might chance to be. And, if she saw Dorothy make a certain signal, then Ozma would know that the little Kansas girl wanted to revisit the Land of Oz, and by means of the Nome

King's magic belt would wish that she might instantly return.

This having been agreed upon, Dorothy bade good-bye to all her friends. Tiktok wanted to go to Australia, too; but Dorothy knew that the machine man would never do for a servant in a civilized country, and the chances were that his machinery wouldn't work at all. So she left him in Ozma's care.

Billina, on the contrary, preferred the Land of Oz to any other country, and refused to accompany Dorothy.

"The bugs and ants that I find here are the finest flavored in the world," declared the yellow hen, "and there are plenty of them. So here I shall end my days; and I must say, Dorothy, my dear, that you are very foolish to go back into that stupid, humdrum world again."

"Uncle Henry needs me," said Dorothy, simply; and every one except Billina thought it was right that she should go.

All Dorothy's friends of the Land of Oz—both old and new—gathered in a group in front of the palace to bid her a sorrowful good-bye and to wish her long life and happiness. After much hand shaking, Dorothy kissed Ozma once more, and then handed her the Nome King's magic belt, saying:

"Now, dear Princess, when I wave my handkerchief, please wish me with Uncle Henry. I'm aw'fly sorry to leave you—and the Scarecrow—and the Tin Woodman—and the Cowardly Lion—and

Tiktok—and—and everybody—but I do **want my** Uncle Henry! So good-bye, all of you."

Then the little girl stood on one of the **big** emeralds which decorated the courtyard, and after looking once again at each of her friends, waved her handkerchief.

*   *   *

"No,' said Dorothy, "I wasn't drowned at all. And I've come to nurse you and take care of you, Uncle Henry, and you must promise to get well as soon as poss'ble."

Uncle Henry smiled and cuddled his little niece close in his lap.

"I'm better already, my darling," said he.

The End

Ozma

THE OZ SERIES BY L. FRANK BAUM

Published by
For Your Knowledge

available from the Ann Arbor Media Group
at Amazon.com and your local retailer

Which ones do you have?